THIS IS NOT YOUR WAR, NICK CARTER, AMERICAN. I WANT NO HARM TO COME TO YOU. GO HOME AND LET US FIGHT OUR WARS OURSELVES.

The street was quiet, deserted. His mind was distracted. That was why the thud on the roof of the car and the following whine froze him for an instant, instead of galvanizing him into action.

The second slug jerked at his coat, and Carter felt a burning sensation across his left arm and wrist.

That moved him. He lurched across the street and then went into a dive toward the opposite walk. He hit the cement with a breath-pounding jolt, digging under his coat for Wilhelmina.

At the same time, a third slug whined off the cement a foot from his head.

But this time he saw the rifle, the orange spray flared even more than normal because of the silencer. It came from an office building across the street, third floor, corner window.

Carter was up and running in the shadows...

NICK CARTER IS IT!

"Nick Carter out-Bonds James Bond."
—*Buffalo Evening News*

"Nick Carter is America's #1 espionage agent."
—*Variety*

"Nick Carter is razor-sharp suspense."
—*King Features*

"Nick Carter has attracted an army of addicted readers . . . the books are fast, have plenty of action and just the right degree of sex . . . Nick Carter is the American James Bond, suave, sophisticated, a killer with both the ladies and the enemy."
— *The New York Times*

FROM THE NICK CARTER
KILLMASTER SERIES

TERMS OF VENGEANCE

KILL MASTER

NICK CARTER

J

JOVE BOOKS, NEW YORK

KILLMASTER #229: TERMS OF VENGEANCE

A Jove Book/published by arrangement with
The Condé Nast Publications, Inc.

PRINTING HISTORY
Jove edition/September 1987

ISBN: 0-515-09214-2

Jove Books are published by The Berkley Publishing Group,
200 Madison Avenue, New York, New York 10016.
The name "JOVE" and the "J" logo
are trademarks belonging to Jove Publications, Inc.

PRINTED IN THE UNITED STATES OF AMERICA

10 9 8 7 6 5 4 3 2 1

Dedicated to the men of the
Secret Service of the
United States of America

PART ONE

ONE

August 1966—Jordan

Outside, the morning heat had already descended on Jordan's capital, Amman. The modern chaos of buses, taxis, and business bustle didn't invade the tenth-floor suite of the Philadelphia Hotel where Nick Carter added ice to three fingers of scotch and sat facing his visitor.

"Drink?" Carter asked.

"No, thank you."

The woman who faced Carter was beautiful in the darkly mysterious way most Middle Eastern women were beautiful. She was young, not more than twenty-five, with a slender, compact figure that was curiously rigid as she sat in a chair leaning toward him.

It was the first time Carter had met her in person, but they had been in constant communication for the last three weeks.

The only name he knew her by was Darva. She was an agent of Mossad, Israeli intelligence. Together, they had

1

been setting up a meeting between Jordan's King Hussein and three representatives of the Israeli government.

It was tricky, very touch and go.

Hussein, tired of the Palestine Liberation Organization's use of Jordan as a jumping-off point for raids into Israel, had broken with the PLO.

There was only one very big hitch. Hussein couldn't get rid of the PLO, nor could he stop their raids. Israel was sending three men to negotiate with Hussein and offer Israeli aid to do just that.

"I assume everything is ready from this end?"

The pupils of her eyes were contracted and cloudy beneath heavy black lashes, and they stared into Carter's face with a fixed intensity that, in his opinion, wasn't quite sane.

But he could forgive her that. An Israeli agent hopping from Tel Aviv to Damascus to Amman—and then running illegally around Jordan—would have to be a little nuts.

"As far as it can be," Carter replied, sipping his drink. "Hussein has agreed to every aspect of the meeting. A car will pick you and the three gentlemen up at the safe house outside the city at midnight."

"And he has guaranteed their safety as long as they are in the palace?"

"Completely." And then he shrugged. "Of course, *outside* the palace . . ."

She drew herself stiffly erect in the deep chair, nervous fingers weaving together in her lap. "That is the chance we all take stepping across the frontier into an Arab country."

Carter nodded. "I know. Where are they now?"

She checked a thin watch on her wrist. "They arrived in the village of Summa under cover of darkness late last night and caught the first bus to Amman this morning. They should be well on the road by now. Our contact in

Summa was to supply them with proper travel papers and dress."

"Such as . . . ?"

"One will be traveling as a rich Lebanese trader from Beirut, another as an imam from the Sinai. A third poses as a schoolteacher from France. He is traveling with a woman posing as his wife."

Carter nodded. "It sounds good. Do they all have good papers?"

"Excellent," she replied firmly.

"And you trust your Summa contact?"

Her lovely lips curved slightly. "As much as we can trust any Arab. He is a Palestinian, but greedy. He needs a corridor across Israel to bring his goods to Haifa and the sea. Because of this he helps us."

"Let's hope his greed remains his prime mover."

"If anything had occurred last night, I would have heard this morning."

"Let's hope so," Carter said, then stood up. "It's a long time until they arrive . . . lunch?"

She stood, obviously gathering herself to leave. "I have much to do. Security is difficult here in Amman. I will ring you the moment they are in the safe house." Without another word, she stalked to the door and left.

Carter's actions after she was gone seemed unconscious. He moved with the precise somnambulism of habit in every motion. With automatic smoothness he pulled a chair to the window. He sat and lit a cigarette, staring down at the bustle of Al Hashimi Street.

There was nothing in his face to show what he was thinking: *Too many PLO ears left in Jordan. This meeting is going to be a disaster.*

• • •

A handsome youth of eight, his olive skin and smoke-gray eyes blending well with the sable darkness of his curly hair, stared broodingly out the bus window at the rocky peaks of the El Sat mountains. In the distance the land leveled out to the valley of the river Jordan, one of the most fertile areas in the world.

Nearby he saw shepherds in dun-colored djellabas urging camels around drawing wells and herding flocks of sheep toward heavier patches of grass, much the same as their ancestors had done two thousand years before. Their clothing against the terrain rendered them nearly invisible to all but the keenest and most knowledgeable eye.

The boy had such an eye.

Beside the boy sat his mother, a beautiful young woman with eyes black as a raven's feather. The similarity of the boy's and woman's aristocratic features could attest to their kinship. She was a tall woman with a fine nose and a firm, sculpted chin. Those who knew the myriad tribes of the Middle East could spot her heritage at a glance. Her bearing and stature were almost regal. She was a Druse, and there were shadows of her ferocious forebears in the flash of her eyes and the set of her chin.

When mother and son spoke, it was in Arabic. But they could converse equally well in French, Spanish, Greek, or Italian.

At the moment, both of them were more interested in the conversation around them than in speaking to each other. The mixture of humanity that populated the bus talked of only one thing, the same thing that all of Jordan talked about: war.

The talk wasn't foreign to the boy. He heard the same diverse points of view discussed constantly in his father's house. His father, Omar, and his uncle, Abu, were brothers only in blood. They differed radically in most every way, but particularly on the issue of Palestine.

His Uncle Abu was a boisterous giant of a man who would fly into wild rages at the mention of anything Israeli. He was a wealthy merchant trader who had made his fortune buying cheap from the ignorant peasants of the interior and selling high in the coastal markets. He viewed Palestine as his own personal property.

The boy's father, while equal to his brother in size, was far different in disposition. He was a quiet, thoughtful man who deplored violence and preached a love of the people and the land rather than a rape of it. Omar Rahman had accepted defeat, and the Israelis.

The war that raged within and without his family confused the boy.

His eyes moved from the scene outside the window to his fellow passengers.

A young, recently married couple occupied the seat in front of him. They spoke in French. The girl had shared some fruit with him earlier, and had marveled at his striking gray eyes as well as his perfect French. The young woman's husband was like the boy's father, soft-spoken with a charming smile. He was to be a teacher in Amman, and he hoped that all his students were as quick and bright as the boy who, at eight, so charmed his wife.

The boy didn't blush. He had heard similar compliments all his young life. He accepted it.

Across the aisle sat a bearded and robed man who emanated the same brand of proud composure as his mother. Only this man, unlike his mother, smothered his regal bearing with arrogance. This man was obviously important, obviously rich, obviously Arab, and most eager to let everyone around him know it.

When asked his name by the boy, he had proclaimed "Caid Haj of Beirut!" as if he were royalty and practically one with Allah Himself.

The boy almost believed him.

Feeling cramped and restless from the long ride, the boy stood to stretch his legs. At that instant, the driver cried out and applied the full force of his leg and foot to the brakes. The bus slid to a gravel-crunching halt, pitching the boy forward the length of the aisle. The driver nearly trampled him as he threw open the door and leaped, cursing, to the ground.

With the other occupants of the bus babbling in chaos, the boy pulled himself up and looked out the broad, mud-streaked front window. He found himself confronted with a makeshift barricade surrounded by armed men; machine guns displayed with pride. The bus driver was chattering and pointing as a few of the men entered the vehicle, knocking the boy back in their haste.

He sat startled in the driver's seat as the men walked slowly up the aisle. They paused at each seat, loudly interrogating the frightened occupants. When they reached the far rear of the bus they started back, only to stop abruptly in the center.

Roughly, they yanked Caid Haj and the French couple from their seats and shoved them forward. The young woman smiled as she passed him. Her husband looked lost, but he also smiled and winked assurance that everything would be all right.

Caid Haj blustered, threatened, and then screamed in real fear as a rifle butt in his back propelled him from the bus into the roadside dust.

The party congregated just outside the door. The boy sat, mesmerized, as he listened to the halting, multilingual conversations. He followed it all. He had as fine an ear for dialects as he did for languages. He recognized the rebels as Palestinians, and shivered.

He heard his mother's voice calling to him, and then the shuffle of her sandals as she moved forward in the aisle. He didn't answer her. The goings-on outside the bus were too fascinating.

The PLO leader, a tall, angular man with a black-bearded face, was loudly questioning Caid Haj.

His only reply was more blustering.

A scar, running from the rebel leader's left earlobe to the point of his chin, suddenly seemed to glow white in his otherwise dark face. With an oath, he smashed the palm of his hand into Caid Haj's face. Blood spurted in its wake, and even before the robed man could cry out in pain, his assailant's boot had found his testicles.

Caid Haj writhed on the ground. The young bride of the schoolteacher ran to his side. She had barely dropped to her knees when she found herself raised and slammed, with a jarring thud, against the side of the bus.

Her husband came to life. He cursed the rebel and rushed toward him, only to suffer the pain of a badly mashed nose. He joined his wife against the bus and was quickly followed by Caid Haj, his hands grasping his groin in pain.

The rebel leader stepped back, calmly lit a cigarette, and began the interrogation all over again.

As he listened to the man, Caid Haj's demeanor changed, the expression in his eyes altering from fear to a hard intensity as he drew himself to his full height and spat on the ground in the front of his tormentors.

Then, from under his robes, he drew a pistol. He fired once, and a red splotch appeared on the dirty white haik of the machine-gun-wielding man nearest him.

Without a sound the man pitched forward, and Caid Haj

swung his gun toward the leader. But before he could fire again, the air was filled with the staccato chatter of gunfire.

The bursts not only found their intended victims, but ripped into the bus as well. People tumbled into the aisle or curled up, hands over their heads, in their seats. Everyone, man and woman alike, was screaming. One man, bearded and dressed in the robes of an imam, half crawled and half ran to the rear of the bus and clawed at the emergency door.

At his ear the boy heard a tiny groan in a voice he recognized. He turned just as his mother fell, the whole right sleeve of her white djellaba stained crimson.

The boy was frozen in both mind and body. He couldn't think or move. It was as though he were an outsider, objectively observing mass murder. Beside the door he could see the torn and bloody bodies of the French schoolteacher, his lovely young wife, and Caid Haj of Beirut. They were grotesquely sprawled across each other as if they had embraced one another even as they embraced death.

Fearful, screaming, wriggling bodies filled the aisle, but no one else seemed wounded. Only his mother who lay, unmoving, at his feet.

The PLO leader, his face a dark mask of emotionless calm, leaped into the bus. The machine pistol in his hand roared, and the imam in the rear screamed his last as the bullets tore his spine to shreds.

Then, just as calmly, the man slung his weapon and knelt beside the fallen woman. The boy watched, impassive, as a knife appeared in the man's hand. He rolled the woman to her back, and raised the knife.

The boy screamed.

"Pig!" he shouted, and threw his small body at the PLO leader's head.

The man turned at the shouted cry just in time to take the full force of the boy's butting skull in his face. Stunned, caught off guard, he fell backward. The knife slipped from his grasp and clattered against the steel floor.

The boy's knees hit and then his hands, one of them over the hilt of the knife. Without even looking down, he grasped and folded it into both his hands. Crawling forward on his knees, still screaming "Pig! Pig! Dirty pig!," he raised the gleaming blade high above his head.

The leader, blood coursing from his ruptured nose into both his eyes, barely managed to roll to his side. He was able to save himself from a killing thrust, but not from injury.

The blade passed through the bicep of his left arm and was saved from entering his body by a rib. Realization that the blow was not a mortal one registered through the haze of the boy's fury. He withdrew the knife and raised if for a second thrust, this time at the man's neck.

But he wasn't quick enough. Again the man rolled, this time into the boy's body. The hand at the end of his long, sinewy arm was flat out as it landed against the side of the boy's head.

The youth tumbled but, like a spring, came to his feet. Now to the haze of fury clouding his eyes was added a loss of equilibrium caused by the stunning blow on his ear. He could barely see the man climbing to his feet before him.

But still he tried. From the height of his own knees he brought the knife up, underhand, toward the rebel's exposed belly.

But it wasn't to be.

His thrust was blocked. He scarcely felt the fist in his own belly before the air left his lungs and pain shot through his whole body from the floorboard gearshift in his back.

Blackness enveloped him but he fought it off. His eyes opened but he couldn't move. The bus was silent save for his own raspy attempts at breathing and the sound of someone shredding fabric.

The man was ripping open his mother's djellaba, and then the dress she wore beneath it. Suddenly his mother was naked to her waist. The brown skin of her right breast looked pale next to the seeping blood.

Gently, his face, even with the bleeding nose, returning to calm detachment, the rebel leader cut her djellaba into strips. He cleaned the wound and then bound it. He then took a cushion from a seat and placed it under her head.

"The wound is not deep. The bullet passed between her arm and her side." He spoke as if he were assuring himself as much as the still cowering people hovering at his shoulder.

Then, taking the knife, he stood and moved forward toward the boy. Much to the boy's surprise, he saw the man's face change expression for the first time since the affair had begun.

He was smiling. It was a cruel smile made slightly grotesque by the drying blood, but nevertheless it was a smile.

"Are you all right, little warrior?"

"My back hurts."

The man turned him over and probed with sensitive fingers. Then he lifted him effortlessly into a seat. "A bruise. You will live to fight more battles." Using the knife, he stripped away his own sleeve and began binding his arm. "And, luckily, so will I."

"I went for your heart."

"How well I know, little one, and you almost succeeded. You are very brave."

The boy managed to gather enough spit in his dry mouth to make a ball, but his aim was poor. He missed the rebel's face and hit his shoulder. "Son of a whore!" the boy hissed.

Instead of anger, the rebel's lips curled into a wider smile. "You curse as well as you fight. Your name?"

"Ja'il Rahman," the boy said proudly.

The man's face changed. His eyes narrowed and darted to the woman on the floor before he spoke again. "You are of the Rahman clan of Summa?"

"My father is Omar and my uncle is Abu."

Suddenly the man pressed the knife into the boy's hand. His eyes fell. The hilt of the knife was inlaid with tiny jewels shaping the star and crescent of Islam.

The man leaned close to the boy's ear. "Should you ever need a friend, little warrior, just show the knife to anyone and you will be taken to Hassan Al-Chir." He jumped from the bus. "You, driver, return to Summa and tell all who will listen that Hassan Al-Chir has killed the Jews who drove us from our homeland! And if more come to conspire with Jordan's king against us, they too will die!"

Then the man, Hassan Al-Chir, was gone. The driver reappeared in his seat and the ancient bus roared to life. They managed to turn around on the narrow road, and as they moved off, a young woman, not more than fourteen, jumped on the front bumper and shouted at them through the windshield.

"A warning and lesson to you all! There is no Israel! Palestine is ours!"

Through the dust the boy could see the rebels, mounted now and already riding single file up into the craggy hills. The three bodies were merely a pile in the roadside dust. The young teacher's blood oozed just like that of Caid Haj. His pretty young wife's body lay across the imam's in the dust.

Four dead. Jews?

The boy, Ja'il Rahman, was even more confused.

He looked down at the knife in his hand.

Little did he know that, in less than twenty-four hours, he would be witness to much more killing.

TWO

Carter ate in his room and smoked and paced. At last, shortly after eleven, the telephone rang.

It was the woman, Darva.

"It was a trap, an ambush. Hassan Al-Chir led it."

The Killmaster felt a lump of lead hit the bottom of his gut. "All three of them?"

"Yes, and the girl. I have seen the bodies on the Amman road. I am going to Summa. Retaliation has already been planned. I am going to find the Rahman pig and get my own revenge."

Carter had lived too long on the edge himself not to recognize a touch of insanity in the voice of another. He recognized it now in the voice of this woman, and he didn't like it. Finding and killing the man who had fingered the three Israeli emissaries was one thing; how it was done was another.

"Wait," he said. "Let me get to the king. This could be the incident that would move the government of Jordan to action without negotiation."

"There is no time," Darva replied, the manic edge clear

in her voice. "You are out of it now, Carter. Go home."

The phone went dead in his hand. Carter dropped it and forced his mind to make a rapid decision.

A raid now on any Jordanian village would give the PLO the leverage they needed to convince the other Arab leaders to put pressure on King Hussein to mount an attack on Israel.

Quickly, with no wasted motion, Carter moved. He changed into dark clothes and slid his arms into a shoulder rig housing the 9mm Luger he affectionately called Wilhelmina. Hugo, a deadly six-inch stiletto, was already in the chamois sheath on his right forearm.

Over it all he pulled a dark gray djellaba and wrapped a *hata* around his head. The scant contents of his traveling bag he left. He knew he wouldn't be coming back, but it didn't matter. The clothing was without labels, and there was nothing else in the bag to identify him as an American, let alone an agent of supersecret AXE.

He could almost sense the tension on the street. Word of the killings must have already reached Amman. And if it had leaked that the victims were Israelis, the populace would be tense waiting for Israeli retaliation.

He walked for several blocks until he found what he wanted: a motorcycle shop. Darva had said that she had seen the bodies on the road. That meant that she was already halfway to Summa. A motorcycle would allow Carter to save time on desolate back roads impassable to an automobile.

Picking the rear door of the shop was child's play. Inside, he found a powerful BMW gassed and ready to go.

Minutes later he was roaring toward the outskirts of Amman.

● ● ●

The car slid to a halt and the motor was cut immediately. In the rear, the woman leaned forward between the two men in the front bucket seats.

"That is the house of Rahman. Yani, take the rear. Meir, you go in the front with me."

The two men exchanged puzzled glances. The woman was their superior, but what she was proposing could well be suicide. The area of Summa they were in was completely controlled by PLO underground.

"Darva, are you sure that this raid has the go-ahead?"

"Do you doubt my order?" she hissed. "Let's go!" She slid from the car and moved toward the house in shadows.

Even with the doubts in their minds, both men were trained to obey. They left the car and followed, flicking off the safeties on the Uzi submachine guns they held.

Ja'il Rahman lay awake in his bed, his eyes wide, his mind full of the day's events.

Upon their return, his uncle Abu had peppered them with questions. The more his mother answered, the more ashen his uncle's face had become.

"They told me they were only going to capture them! Hassan Al-Chir promised me there would be no killing!"

The boy had listened, wide-eyed, until his mother and father realized he was in the room. He was hustled off to bed, but through a crack in his door he continued to listen to their conversation.

"They will come, Abu," his father said. "You must hide."

"See what your greed and your treachery has brought upon our heads, Abu Rahman!" His mother's voice was bitter.

"Silence!" his father snapped. "What is done is done. Abu, you must not be here if they come."

"The PLO will guard me. I have done them a service."

"Perhaps, but I would rather have them guard you somewhere else," his father said dryly. "You can stay in the cellar of Salamel until we are sure it is safe. I will send word."

Ja'il heard his father shuffle from the room, and then his mother's voice.

"You are a pig, Abu."

"Be quiet, woman!"

"You play the PLO and the Israelis against each other and endanger us all."

"I do what I must do. Here, take this pistol. You may need it."

His uncle stole away into the night, and minutes later someone from the camp of Hassan Al-Chir arrived to watch over them.

Now Ja'il could hear his father and their guard talking in hushed tones in the room directly below him. The boy slid his hand beneath his pillow and curled his fingers around the jeweled hilt of the dagger given him by Hassan Al-Chir.

His father had said Hassan Al-Chir was a madman, a wanton killer using a war to satisfy his own bloodlust.

His uncle said Al-Chir was a great man, a freedom fighter.

His mother said they should all move to Paris, and then she went to bed.

Suddenly Ja'il heard the crash of glass in the front of the house. At the same time, gunfire erupted amid screams of agony.

Instinctively, he clutched the dagger and rushed from his tiny loft. At the top of the ladder leading into the large room of the house, he froze.

The PLO guard and another man were sprawled in the

kitchen doorway, blood puddling beneath them. His father
was on his knees in the middle of the room, clutching his
side.

A man, all in black, crouched at the broken front window, staring out, a gun in his hands.

And by the door stood a wild-eyed woman, also in
black and training a submachine gun on his father.

"You are Rahman!" the woman screamed.

"I am Omar Rahman."

"Where is Abu Rahman?"

"I do not know."

"You lie!" the woman said, her voice now a hysterical
screech.

"Abu is my brother," his father said, crawling painfully
to his feet.

The woman lowered the muzzle of the Uzi and fired.
The bullets tore across the floor and into Omar Rahman's
legs.

Ja'il screamed out as his father fell, but it was nothing
compared to the ear-splitting shriek of his mother as she
entered from her bedroom, a raised pistol in her hand.

Through the mist of tears in the boy's eyes he saw the
pistol buck and spit flame again and again. The body of the
black-clad man at the window seemed to be on strings as
he danced backward into the wall and slowly sank to the
floor, leaving a wide smear of red on the plaster.

And then the Uzi in the woman's hand was chattering.
Ja'il saw his mother stagger, clutch her bloody middle, and
fall.

The boy went wild. He leaped from his perch and ran
blindly toward the woman. Before she could bring the Uzi
around, Ja'il buried the dagger's blade into her belly.

She crashed against the wall, freeing the blade. He
lunged again, but the snout of the Uzi came around, strik-

ing him in the side and knocking him into the open door.

"Run, Ja'il, run . . . now!"

It was his father's voice. The boy stared at his father, his mother, and at the rest of the carnage.

"Run, Ja'il!"

Suddenly the Uzi barked again, shattering the door-frame behind him and riddling his back with painful splinters.

He ran headlong into the street. He had gone only a few steps when a man in a dark djellaba riding a huge black motorcycle was in his path.

"No, Darva, no!" the man shouted in English.

Ja'il looked over his shoulder. The woman had staggered through the door and fallen. But she was coming up on one knee and raising the gun.

"Get on!" the man barked in Arabic as the bullets slammed into the sidewalk behind him.

Ja'il was stunned, frozen. Then a powerful arm was lifting him and he was settled into the saddle behind the man.

"Hang on!"

The machine roared and the rear tire screamed as they lurched forward.

Ja'il looped his arms around the man's waist and locked his fingers tightly as more bullets from the Uzi chased them down the dusty street.

Gently, Carter turned the boy onto his stomach. He was wearing only a pair of shorts and the shirt to a pair of pajamas. The back of the pajama top was torn to shreds and bloody. Carefully, using Hugo, Carter cut it away.

No single wound was serious, but he could count over fifty splinters of various sizes embedded in the boy's back.

In the light of false dawn, he went to work with the

stiletto, easing the splinters out one by one. It was good that the boy had passed out. The removal of several of the more deeply embedded ones would have caused excruciating pain if he were conscious.

This done, the Killmaster tore his djellaba in half. He soaked it in a trickling stream nearby and bathed the cuts. Because of the amount of bleeding, there was little chance of infection.

Tearing the other half of the djellaba into strips, he made a grass poultice and covered the boy's back. He was just finishing the last binding when he realized that the boy had awakened.

One cold gray eye was staring at him from between long, blue-black lashes.

"You repair my body in order to torture it?"

"Why would I want to torture you?"

"To find where my uncle Abu hides. That is why they came . . . to find my uncle. Are you a Jew?"

Carter was somewhat taken aback. The boy was calm considering the situation, and he spoke in a cold, detached way.

"I am American."

"An American Jew? America is full of Jews."

Carter sighed. "I am an American who works for my government. My name is Carter, Nick Carter, and you can trust me. I mean you no harm."

The boy sat up. Though the pain in his back had to be severe, he barely winced.

"That is my knife."

Carter looked down at the jeweled dagger he had taken from the boy's hand and stuck in his belt. He pulled it out and handed it to the boy.

"What is your name?"

"Ja'il. I am the son of Omar Rahman."

Now the picture was a little clearer. Carter managed to keep his face expressionless when he spoke again.

"Tell me what happened . . . everything."

Ja'il sat, staring directly into Carter's eyes. It was as if he were reliving everything before he could speak of it. And when he did speak, it was in the same calm, detached voice.

Carter noted that, even relating the worst of the details, the boy's face did not change nor did he shed a single tear.

Shock, the Killmaster guessed, or worse.

From the boy's description, Carter surmised that it had been a total wipeout on both sides. If Darva's wound had been as the boy remembered, she had probably bled to death.

"Why?" Ja'il asked.

"Why?" Carter repeated. "I don't think you would understand."

"I am wise for my years. My father has told me so, often. Why?"

Again Carter took a deep breath and tried to explain. He told the boy the real identities of those he had seen on the bus. He explained what he guessed had been his uncle's part in it.

"And the woman? Well, Ja'il, all I can say about the woman is that she went a little mad."

"Then it is as my mother said. All this was caused by my uncle's greed and treachery."

"I'm afraid it goes far beyond that."

"No matter. I will have to kill my uncle."

The words jerked Carter's head up. It was in the youth's eyes, in the set of his young jaw.

He meant every word he said.

"Right now, you're in no shape to kill anyone," Carter said, standing. "Where do you have family?"

"I have no family."

"Then I'll take you with me. I'm going north into Lebanon, Beirut. There are people there who—"

"No."

"What?"

Ja'il stood. He gazed around him and then faced Carter. "These are the caves of Modor. There is the road to Lebanon, but you should not go that way. Those hills are alive with the men of Hassan Al-Chir. They would stop you and kill you. Go south, cross the frontier into Israel, there. It is the safer way to Lebanon."

"And you, Ja'il, what will you do?"

"I will survive."

"Ja'il how old are you?"

"A lifetime older than I was at this time yesterday." He moved to the mouth of the cave, stood for a few moments staring out over the valley and the river Jordan, and then turned back to face Carter. "You have saved my life, Nick Carter, American. I thank you."

"Listen, son . . ."

"Good-bye, Nick Carter. Be careful as you ride. Stop for no one." He turned and started walking down the hillside.

Carter moved to the edge of the cave and watched.

In the remnants of the djellaba, the shorts, and barefoot, his small, frail body was the most pathetic figure Carter had ever seen.

But he didn't call out or try to stop him. He knew it would be useless just from the way the boy walked, his shoulders squared, his head straight forward and his chin high. He watched until the small figure disappeared in the rocks and the rising heat haze.

I will survive.

And somehow Carter knew he would.

PART TWO

THREE

Now

The bar was in the Nazaret section of Valencia, near the port. There was nothing ornate or pretentious about it. It had the usual long counter, the mirror and array of bottles behind it, and about thirty tables.

Carter slid onto one of the barstools at exactly nine o'clock. Because of the early hour there were few customers: two more men at the bar, a few couples, and the usual array of hookers, as well as three secretary types.

Carter guessed that the secretary types were on the hunt, moonlighting. A little flat-back time for extra income wasn't frowned on in Spain.

"Señor?" The bartender was a chubby little man with bland eyes, a mustache, and ring-around-the-collar.

"Whiskey, double, no ice."

"Sí, señor."

While the bartender poured, Carter cased the women, face after face, and gave up.

"The contact is a woman," AXE Madrid had said.

"Once you're in Valencia and set up, go to a flamenco bar called Los Quatros Palomas at exactly nine the night before the party."

"Description?" Carter had asked.

"None. All we have is a name . . . Ynez."

None of the women he currently perused in the bar looked like she would be Ynez.

The whiskey came just as a small spotlight hit the stage at the end of the room. A dark-eyed young woman stepped into it, carrying a guitar. She was slim and supple as a reed, with jet-black hair pulled back from her face. She was wearing a peasant blouse and a ruffled flamenco skirt that was weighted so it swirled around her as she moved.

"Is that the show?" Carter asked.

"Oh, no, señor. The flamenco starts at eleven. This girl plays until then."

Carter nodded and sipped his whiskey. The girl played very well. He had a hard time taking his eyes from her when more customers entered.

She finished her first set in a half hour and stood to solid applause, considering the small amount of people in the place.

"Muchas gracias. Ynez thanks you all."

She was looking right at Carter when she said it. She left the stage, and minutes later reappeared in the room, a dark shawl around her shoulders. As she passed Carter, she gave him one more quick look.

"Another, señor?" the bartender asked.

"No, thanks. I think I'll get some air."

The bartender sighed deeply and swabbed the bar. "Ah, señor, that one will do you no good. She has a boyfriend. A very mean boyfriend."

"Keep the change," Carter chuckled. "I'm not interested . . . too young."

Carter was aware of the disappointed look on the bartender's face as he walked out the door. He probably got a cut from the B girls and the secretaries.

The dead end was to the left, beside the water. Carter fished a cigarette from his pocket and headed that way. He was in the deepest part of the shadows when she joined him.

"Do you have another of those?"

"They are Zelos, Turkish, very strong."

"I don't mind."

She took one of the cigarettes. Carter snapped his lighter and held the flame steady.

She looked even younger up close and the face was more striking, clean, and although not pretty, it was somehow strong, intelligent, and well poised.

"You are . . .?"

"Carter. Nick Carter."

"And you have proof?"

He flipped his wallet and the lighter again. The way she studied his credentials told him that she knew what to look for.

"Good. You have access to Señor Araujo's gala as a guest."

"I do. But from what I hear, his galas generally turn out to be expatriate orgies."

She chuckled, but not with a lot of mirth. "This is true. Señor Vincente Araujo has a weakness for American widows and wives. I assume you do not attend alone?"

"No," Carter drawled, "I'll be the escort of Monique Leveque. She is—"

"A gossip writer for *Paris Jet Set*. I know, I have read some of her articles. The woman is obsessed with sex."

Carter managed to suppress a smile. *If you only knew,* he thought.

She rummaged in the pocket of her skirt as she spoke again. "You have the money, in cash?"

"Three hundred and fifty thousand, in cash, and two passports. All they need are photographs."

"Here," she said, handing him a folded slip of paper. "This is the floor plan of the house. At exactly midnight, slip away. The door to the wine cellar will be marked and unlocked. At the bottom, just under the stairs, there are three wine casks. The center one is marked Moulney '47. the cask is empty and the top is unsealed. Put the money in there and leave."

"Your man is not very trusting."

"He cannot afford to be. Betraying Hassan Al-Chir is writing one's own death warrant."

"Three hundred and fifty thousand is a lot of money."

Her head jerked up, the innocent features now in a grimace of fear. "A list of all of Hassan Al-Chir's world-wide terrorist nets and operatives—with names, addresses, and pictures—is worth ten times that much."

"I hope so," Carter replied, "but I would like to know who I'm paying."

"You are paying a man who has been a courier for Al-Chir for years. Every name on the list is active and accurate."

They both fell silent, the only sound the lapping of the water against the jetty and some far-off lonesome fog-horns.

At last she flipped her cigarette into the water and spoke again. "After you put the money in the cask, rejoin the party. At three o'clock, and not before, you should be able to slip away again."

"And then?"

"And then . . ." She paused uncertainly, and then continued. "And then there is no more. We crawl into a hole and you have the power to bring a madman to ground."

"Is that why your friend is betraying Al-Chir? Because he is a madman?"

"That is one of many reasons, but the main one. Even Arafat and most of the Palestinians would like some kind of peace now. Not Al-Chir. He makes war only because he is obsessed with the power and glory it gives him. That is why only the most rabid of fanatics follow him."

She turned and started away. Carter fell in step beside her. "You know I could be of more solid help if you and he would let me."

"No. We have planned this for months. It is the safest way. That is why you must follow the instructions for the exchange to the letter."

She turned into the door of the bar and Carter continued on up the street. It took five minutes to find a prowling taxi.

"*Saler Sol, por favor.*"

"*Sí, señor.*" The taxi rocked ahead and Carter spotted the driver looking at him in the rearview. "It is good you leave down here early, señor. The Nazaret is no good place for tourist late in the night."

"I'm not a tourist," Carter growled. "I'm a secret agent."

The driver laughed.

The Killmaster closed the door of Suite 804 behind him and Monique Leveque met him halfway down the steps into the sunken sitting room. She kissed him on the mouth, then reached up and rubbed some of her lipstick from the corner of his lip.

"Thank God you are back, Nicky, I was dying of lonesomeness." Abruptly, she came into his arms, flattening her well-endowed chest against him. "Did you spy good?"

"I'm a travel writer, remember?"

"Of course you are, and I am still a virgin. Do you want a drink?"

"Yeah."

He watched the play of her thighs as she moved toward the bar. She wore a green robe of some satiny material that danced along with every muscle.

"Your tryst was successful?"

"It was," Carter said, shrugging from his jacket and the shoulder rig. "Are we still on for the orgy tomorrow night?"

"*Mais oui*. Vincente loves to look down the front of my dress even though I am not a rich American expatriate widow. Here."

She pressed the glass of good scotch into his hand, and her body followed.

"I hope you are in the mood for love," she purred, nibbling on his ear.

"We made love this afternoon."

"So? We made love this morning and last night. You should not keep score, Nicky. It takes the fun out of it."

"You're a nymphomaniac."

"I know. Everyone should have a purpose in life."

Carter gave up and laughed aloud. Monique was truly a joy to be around.

She had given up a promising career as a nightclub singer when she decided it was silly telling gossip reporters about her wild life and then having them get paid to write it. Particularly when she found out that some of them got paid as well or better than she did for much less work.

At last they unglued themselves and Carter slipped to the sofa. Monique sat just across, her slender ankles together, her scent sharp with femininity. She perched, drink to her lips, as if this were the moment that made her day.

"Was she beautiful?"

"Who?"

"The woman you saw tonight."

"How did you know it was a woman?"

"Her perfume is on that piece of paper in your breast pocket."

Carter chuckled. *"You* should be the spy."

"Never, I detest violence! And, speaking of violence..." She picked up the shoulder rig and the Luger with just the tips of her fingers and headed for the bedroom. "Do you mind if I hang this loathsome thing out of sight?"

It wasn't a question, so Carter didn't answer. Instead he concentrated on her beauty of movement.

"I think Monique Leveque can help us on this one. You know her, Carter?"

"Met her only once."

"She has a lot of contacts, done some damned fine intelligence-gathering for French internal security."

Carter knew the story. About two years earlier, Monique had overheard talk of an arms smuggling deal into Marseille and passed it on to the SDECE in Paris. After that she had just continued to pass along information, and now and then do an active turn.

Carter hadn't known her well when she had met his plane in Madrid a week before. They had talked and laughed over lunch without her asking—or him offering—what the real story of the mission constituted.

By three o'clock that afternoon they had been in bed, together. With Monique, the last week had practically been a vacation.

Now, tonight, began the real work.

"Nicky, darling, do you want to eat out?" she called from the bedroom.

"I suppose so. Don't call me darling."

"Why not?"

"It makes me sound like one of your jet-set gigolos."

Tomorrow night, with any luck, Carter would have the worldwide terrorist network of Hassan Al-Chir in his pocket. And while antiterrorist squads broke up the net, Carter would go after Al-Chir himself.

The girl had been right. Al-Chir was a madman. And Carter would, in this case, be only too happy to exercise the designation his agency had given him and that Monique Leveque knew nothing about: Killmaster.

"Nicholas . . . *dear* . . ."

Carter grunted to his feet and crossed to the bedroom door. "Yeah?"

"Are you sure you want to go out to eat?"

She lay on the bed, her ankles crossed, her hands behind her head, her martini on her belly.

She was stark naked.

"Not particularly."

Carter was naked himself by the time he reached the bed and slipped in beside her.

Her breasts were roundly shaped, mature, the right a bit fuller than the left. Large dark nipples wrinkled themselves erect. In the dim light he could see her soft, dark triangle, the flat sheaths of muscle above it promising more than the usual sensations.

"You want me?" she murmured.

"You're going to spill your martini."

She cupped her breasts with both hands, an offering. "Nice?"

Carter wanted to smile but matched her seriousness. "Nice," he replied, his body tightening.

Suddenly she reached out and ran her finger down his chest. She moved closer, kissing him on the neck, gliding her tongue around his ear.

His hands found her solid thighs, massaging them,

slowly sliding up to her hips and resting there.

Then she was above him, her hands all over his body. "You know what?"

"What?" he growled.

"No one who ever saw you naked with all these scars would believe that you're a travel writer, *cheri.*"

"Then," Carter said, trying to roll her over, "we'll keep it just between ourselves."

She held her position above him. "No," she murmured, "let me."

She slid down the bed and placed her lips on his belly. He was pushing up against her now, but she teased him.

And then she wasn't teasing anymore and Carter was gritting his teeth to retain control.

It was going to be a long night. And he didn't mind at all.

FOUR

"Nice quiet little party," Carter said wryly as he maneuvered the rented Audi into a narrow space and killed the engine.

Monique Leveque chortled throatily with her beautiful head thrown back. *"Oui, cheri,* just like the last night of carnival in Rio! Shall we, as you Americans say, dive in?"

"Let's."

Carter moved around to the passenger side of the Audi and helped her out. She was ravishingly sexy in a figure-fitting, practically backless, low-cut black gown with narrow rhinestone straps. The dress made the whole a packet of superfemininity, displaying every curve and lots of skin.

"Aren't you slightly underdressed?" Carter grinned.

"Ah, Nicky, wait until you see the women at this party!"

They paused for a second at the seawall. Behind them, soft moonlight caressed the rolling sea. Above them, a hundred steps up, Vincente Araujo's grand villa sprawled across the hillside. Between them and the house were terraced gardens blazing with color and scent. The walls of the villa that weren't glass were draped with blooming bougainvillaea, and every window blazed with light.

"Nice little pad," Carter quipped.

"He bought it when prices were right, during Franco."

The music of a *pase doble* and loud laughter hit them through the open doors of the marbled patio leading into the house.

"You know the scene," Carter whispered from the side of his mouth as they moved into a huge room of milling people and glowing chandeliers. "Introduce me around and then let me float."

"Monique, my darling, at last you've arrived . . . the party can now begin!"

"Our host," Monique whispered, and stepped from Carter's side into the arms of Rudolph Valentino had he lived to see sixty.

Vincente Araujo was still Latin-lover-good-looking, with gray hair smoothed back, a square, executive-type jaw, and a deep booming voice. He was dressed in a thousand-dollar tuxedo with real diamond studs.

He kissed Monique all over, patted her fanny, and turned to Carter. "Ah, Monique's latest amour."

"This is Nick, darling. Nick, Vincente Araujo."

"How do you do?"

The man was good. He hardly winced as Carter came just short of breaking his hand.

"I'll do better with a fresh drink. Have fun, both of you. And, Monique . . . be sure to write scandalous things about me and the party!"

He moved away and they mingled. The ratio was about four women to every man, and Carter met most of them without any names registering. Only one, a tall blonde on the long side of forty with more of her out of a dress than in it, made him blink.

Monique introduced her as Nora Pembrook. They chatted inanely for a minute or two and parted, with Nora patting Carter's butt on the way by.

"Very healthy lady," he commented. "I think she likes me."

"Don't get your hopes up," Monique chuckled. "She did that to get to me. Actually, anything over eighteen she throws back. Oh, excuse me, darling, I see someone who just became the center of a scandal. Later."

She moved off and Carter milled, his eyes taking in the men, one by one. Nary a one of them looked like a Middle Eastern terrorist.

"A canapé, señor?"

A white-jacketed waiter was waving a tray of toothpick-speared mouthfuls under Carter's nose.

"Uh . . . sure . . ." Carter's hand wavered over the tray.

"Eel on the left, squid on the right."

"Uh, no, thanks," Carter said. "But where's the bar? I'd like something a little stronger than champagne."

The waiter smiled. "You are American. There are ham sandwiches on the buffet, there. The bar is opposite."

"Thanks." He headed for the bar. "Scotch whiskey, no ice."

"Sí, señor."

By the time Carter got his drink he sensed someone just behind him and to his right, staring. He turned to face a dark-haired young man with movie-star-type looks and a build that belonged in the Olympics.

"Pardon me for staring, but haven't we met before?"

"I don't think so," Carter said, "and I rarely forget a face."

The man nodded and extended his hand. "Gerald Raymond. Perhaps it was a long time ago, or I am mistaken."

Carter took the hand. The grip was firm, radiating an

intense power from just the touch. That same power was in the man's chilly eyes as they bored into Carter's.

"Nick Carter."

"Ah, an American. I wouldn't have known," he said, switching to English. "Your Spanish is excellent."

"As is your English."

Raymond nodded. "My father was English, my mother Israeli. I was born in Tel Aviv."

So much, Carter thought, for Gerald Raymond being his terrorist turncoat.

But still, he was thus far the only man at the party who had shown any interest in Carter.

"I pride myself on accents," the Killmaster said. "Oxford?"

"Cambridge," the other man said with a smile. "But I speak several languages and I'm afraid it dilutes the accent."

Carter was about to say more, when a chunky woman with too much blond hair for her age oozed onto Raymond's arm.

"Gerry, baby, this friggin' party's like a deflated blimp. Come dance with me." Her voice was husky with booze and her accent was sloppy Long Island.

"Elvira Wertz . . . Nick Carter."

The husky-voiced woman looked Carter over and dismissed him. "Hi. Let's dance, Gerry, honey."

"Excuse us," Raymond said, and then whispered in passing, "duty calls."

Carter watched the unlikely pair move into the center of the room, where Elvira enveloped the young man like an octopus swallows its prey.

To each his own, Carter thought, and went in search of Monique Leveque.

He found her in a circle around a very drunk young

woman doing a terrible imitation of a flamenco dance.

"Monique . . ."

"Ah, Nick, just in time. Daphne is about to go into her little act. She does it at every party."

"Monique, that matinee idol dancing with the mini-blimp . . ."

"Gerald Raymond," she replied. "The mini-blimp, as you call her, is Elvira Wertz. Her husband is Wertz Plastics. He gives her a fortune to stay out of the country and his sight."

"Odd couple. What about him?"

"English, pops up every once in a while at parties like this all over the world." She shrugged. "That's about it."

"Does he specialize in fat, rich women?"

"Nicky, with his looks? He can have any woman he wants."

"Then he has money?"

"I suppose," she said and shrugged. "At least he moves around a lot, and in these circles. That takes money."

"I thought you knew everything about everyone."

"Only the scandalous ones, darling. Oh, look, Daphne is reaching her peak."

Carter turned back to the center of the circle. Daphne had dropped the top of her dress to bare two very large, very full breasts. She was currently in the process of slithering her dress down over her hips, to the urgings of the men who were being urged by the women to urge Daphne.

Cater checked his watch. It was three minutes to twelve. Practically the whole room had joined Daphne's circle.

It was a good time to slip away.

The door was where it was supposed to be. Carter found the top step in the darkness and closed the door behind him. Using a penlight, he descended into the cavernous wine cellar beneath the villa. Racks of bottles and huge casks seemed to go on forever. Just one sweep across one rack and he could see that the vintage and vineyard of that rack would have fed a small Third-World country for a year.

The three casks were in place. Carter twisted the lid from the center one and found it empty. Quickly, he pulled his shirt from his pants and unfastened the money belt from his middle. The smell from the cask brought a smile to his lips as he dropped the belt.

He might be able, later, to find out who his man was by the smell that would stick after handling the belt.

At the top of the stairs he opened the door a crack and peered through. As soon as a buxom maid balancing a tray passed, he slipped out.

The party in the main room was now in full swing.

Daphne was *au naturel* except for a pair of spike heels that dug into the priceless veneer of a seventeenth-century tabletop on which she danced. Vincente Araujo didn't seem to mind. He stood as close to the twirling nude body as he could get, and smiled benignly.

Carter slipped to Monique's side in the circle. "What does she do for an ending?"

"One of two things," Monique said. "Throw up or pass out."

"Amusing," Carter groaned, checking the crowd. "The party seems to have thinned out."

"Not really," the woman said, and chuckled. "There are fourteen bedrooms on the second and third floors. At this moment I rather imagine all of them are occupied. Oops, there she goes."

Carter looked. Daphne had swooned off the table into the arms of two men. They laid her out gently on a nearby sofa, and headed for the bar to freshen their drinks. The

other members of the audience drifted away in search of
something new to amuse them.

"Let's get some air," Carter said.

Monique slid her arm under his jacket and around his
waist. "You're thinner."

He nodded. "It's done. I just hope Uncle Sam hasn't
been taken."

The Killmaster tried not to be obvious as he checked his
watch every fifteen minutes. It was just a little after one
o'clock, and he was bored. He had a feeling Monique felt
the same way, and it would be nearly two hours before he
could collect the papers.

They were sitting in the rear gardens just beneath the
patio, listening to the music from inside. Carter was about
to make a trip into the house and the bathroom, when all
hell broke loose.

It was a dull and growing roar, and then the full burst of
the explosion.

Carter whirled to see glass spray from the cellar windows, and then smoke spiral out and rise in the night sky
like a graceful dancer.

Then everyone was on his feet, running outside in
panic. People were pouring from the house to the patio.
From the screams and shouts, Carter guessed they were
also fleeing the house from the front doors and side exits.

"Nick, what is it?" Monique asked, gripping his arm.

"I'd guess a bomb."

"Mon Dieu . . ."

"Stay clear but keep your eyes open. Try to see if anyone leaves in a hurry."

He ran up the steps and across the patio. At the doors he
had to fight the mass of people trying to get out. At last he

made it and sprinted toward the kitchen area.

He yanked open the door to the wine cellar. Heat, smoke, and dust struck his face.

The buxom maid suddenly appeared in the hallway, screaming. Carter grabbed her by the shoulders and shook her until she quieted.

"Listen," he hissed, "find your *patrón*. Have him call the Guardia. Do you understand?"

She nodded dumbly.

"Then hurry! Run!"

She scurried away, and Carter went down what was left of the stairs. There was no need for light. Through the smoke and dust, a sharp flame was growing where the three wine casks had been.

Hurriedly, Carter raced around the walls until he found a fire extinguisher. Thankfully it worked, and in minutes the flame was out.

Then, using his penlight, he searched through the chaos.

It didn't take long.

From what clothing was left on the mangled corpse, he could guess that it was the waiter. A quick perusal told him as much as he needed to know.

The bomber had taken the money belt and planted the explosive device in the cask, the detonator triggered to the lid. When the waiter had lifted it, boom.

Carter could find no scraps of paper or a packet. Quickly he scoured the rest of the cellar, and found out why.

There was a door at the far side of the cellar away from the blast. It was open, as was the second door above, which was level with the ground.

The bomber had obviously taken the money belt, planted his device, and waited until the waiter came down.

After the explosion, he had gathered the papers and made his escape.

The Killmaster went up the steps and emerged in a small garden beside the house. There were two gravel paths, one leading around toward the rear, and one to the side entrance leading to the kitchen.

Carter checked that door and found it unlocked. Chances were good that in the aftermath of the explosion no one would have seen him, even if he had escaped through the kitchen.

Carter took the second path back to the tabled area in the rear of the house beneath the patio.

People were milling around, stunned and jabbering.

He found Monique. "Has anyone called the Guardia?"

"Yes," she said, nodding, "they are on the way. Was it . . . ?"

"Yeah," Carter growled, "he's in pieces. Has anyone tried to leave?"

"Good Lord, yes. Half the guests raced for their cars right away."

"Shit. Here are the keys to the Audi. Stick around here and try to make a mental note of who's left and their reactions. Also, stay close to the Guardia officer and note what they find."

"You?"

"I'm going to break some very bad news to to a lady named Ynez."

He moved away quickly through the gardens. Just as he reached the outer perimeter wall of the gardens, hooting sirens and flashing blue lights went screaming by.

When he was sure that they had all passed, Carter scaled the wall and dropped to the other side.

For the next ten minutes he jogged until he could safely

double back to the beach road.

Once there, he walked calmly until he found a taxi.

The bar and the tables of Los Quatros Palomas were jammed. Carter shouldered his way to a place near the stage, where he sipped a drink until he could catch her eye.

Just his presence told her worlds. Her eyes opened wide and her face drained of color. Her trained fingers went to stone on the guitar, bringing a glowering look from the male singer at her side and the woman dancing.

Carter rolled his eyes to the door.

Ynez nodded, and he made his way through the crowd. Outside, the night was much as it had been before, damp, foggy, with the sounds of the water lapping eerily against the pier.

Five minutes later he heard the music stop, and shortly after that the sound of her heels on the walk.

Then she was there, her lower lip trembling as she stared up at him, clutching the shawl around her shoulders.

"He's dead?"

Carter nodded. "A bomb. Probably one of Al-Chir's people was at the party. There was nothing I could do."

He fell in step beside the girl and they walked in silence toward the dead end and the iron railing.

"I'm sorry," he said. "I have a feeling it would not have happened except for me."

Ynez shook her head impatiently. "No," she said in a breathless way, "it would have happened even if we had gotten the money and disappeared. They would have found us. I think he knew that."

"Who was he?"

"His real name was Yusef Modina. We met at university in Beirut." She clenched the damp iron guardrail and bit her lip. "I didn't know until a few months ago that he was involved with Al-Chir. I was one of the other reasons he wanted out."

She wept for a moment, quietly, and Carter kept his mouth shut until she had dried her eyes. He handed her a cigarette and lit one himself.

"If you don't want to talk about it, I won't press you. But you might still be a great help."

She nodded brusquely. "Why not? But I am afraid I know very little."

"Also, you are probably in a great deal of danger yourself."

She turned toward him, letting the light fall across her face. It was a very young, very unhappy face.

"I think not," she said slowly. "Not now. They didn't know about me. Yusef saw to that."

Carter didn't answer for a moment. He didn't agree with her. He guessed that Yusef had been fingered through her without her even knowing about it. "I would like to take you someplace where men who know how to make you remember could ask you questions."

"You think I might know something and not realize it?"

"Yes. And then, if you wish, I can have you sent anywhere in the world where you think you would be safe."

She thought for a moment. "I have an uncle in England. My mother was English. She met my father while she was a student in Barcelona."

"Then England it is. What do you say?"

Ynez turned her eyes, glistening with tears in the green light, up at him and bit her lower lip ever so slightly. Her mouth was full and sensitive, and more than a little sensual.

"Yusef truly believed in the Palestinian cause. He said it

was men like Al-Chir who prostituted it."

"Then you'll help me find Al-Chir and put him out of business?"

"I'll try."

"Then come along. We're going to Madrid. I just have to leave word for someone at my hotel."

At the head of the alley they found a vacant taxi. Carter gave the driver instructions, and both of them settled back into the seat. They were nearly to the the hotel before Ynez spoke.

"There is one man, an extension of Al-Chir, really, who does his killing. Yusef spoke of him often, but never saw him. He intimated that no one but Al-Chir ever saw him. But that made no difference; everyone feared him. Al-Chir made sure of that."

"Does he have a name?"

"Yes, but it is probably a code name. Yusef said that Al-Chir always called him Ja'il."

"I'll check it against our files of known terrorists," Carter said. "I've never heard the name, but that doesn't mean he isn't on file somewhere."

Monique was at the hotel. A half hour later, the three of them were in the Audi racing for Madrid.

FIVE

"So she was of some help?" Monique said, mashing her cigarette in the ashtray and sipping her coffee.

"A little," Carter replied. "We know from Yusef's travels that Hassan Al-Chir is probably headquartered in or somewhere around Tripoli. We know that if he travels at all it is to somewhere in Tunisia to meet with this Ja'il."

"And from the sound of this Ja'il, it is really he who deserves the legend that Hassan Al-Chir has built up for himself."

Carter nodded. "It's to be expected. It would be impossible for Al-Chir to be in all the places he is supposed to be, and do a tenth of the things he is supposed to do. It would stand to reason that he would have a trained assassin and field leader like this Ja'il to do the hard work for him."

"And Ja'il is a mystery?"

"Completely," Carter said. "There's nothing in any file on him. But at least we can be fairly sure now that he exists."

They fell silent. They were sitting at a sidewalk table at a café across from their Madrid hotel. On the stucco wall behind them, a poster showing a bullfighter in his suit of lights advertised the next day's card at the Plaza de Toros.

From a nearby record store came the sound of gypsy music, with a man wailing at the top of his voice to his lost love.

Monique's eyes wavered on the poster and came to rest on Carter. "You're sure you don't want to take a few more days? I could stay. We could go to the bullfights tomorrow."

Carter shook his head. "No, Washington says come home quick. They have something else for me that comes up in a week or so."

"Pity." She smiled sadly. "We do have a good time together."

"That we do," Carter mused, sipping from his cup of strong Spanish coffee. "But you yourself said Paris couldn't wait."

"Paris can always wait if I want it to." She paused, taking another cigarette from her case. Carter lit it. "Where is the girl, Ynez, now?"

Carter checked his watch. "About halfway to London. She has an uncle somewhere in the countryside. He's her mother's brother, practically raised her. She'll be safe there."

They both nodded. It was small talk now, and they both knew it. The mission had failed, and they both knew it. Hassan Al-Chir's worldwide network would stay intact, and everyone was powerless to do anything about it until another chink could be discovered in his armor.

It was almost with relief that Monique spotted her driver and stood. "You don't want to ride with me to the airport?"

"No," Carter said. "My plane is two hours after yours. I'll check in with Central here and turn in the Audi."

She nodded and leaned her cheek forward to be kissed. "Until next time, *cheri*."

"Until next time," he replied.

"And in the meantime, you have my Paris number."

He patted his breast pocket and grinned. "Close to my heart. *Au revoir*, Monique."

"*Au revoir*, Nicky . . . darling."

Carter watched the limo until it was out of sight, dropped some bills on the table, and crossed the street to the hotel.

"Figure my bill, will you? I'll be checking out."

"*Sí, señor*."

In his room, Carter packed what few toilet articles he had left out, and left a tip for the maids.

Back in the lobby, he paid the bill.

"Oh, Señor Carter, this was in your box."

"Thank you." Carter took the envelope and ripped it open as he left the hotel:

> THIS IS NOT YOUR WAR, NICK CARTER, AMERICAN. I WANT NO HARM TO COME TO YOU. GO HOME AND LET US FIGHT OUR WARS OURSELVES.

The Killmaster dropped his bag and raced back to the desk.

"What is it, Señor Carter?"

"The envelope you just gave me . . ."

"*Sí, señor?*"

"Who left it?"

"It was left with my assistant, señor. One moment."

The man disappeared behind a partition, and seconds later reappeared with a young woman.

"I am sorry, señor, but I didn't see the person who left the note. I was busy and I found it on the counter and put it in your box. Is there something wrong?"

"No . . . no, thank you."

Outside, Carter pocketed the note and retrieved his bag. As he walked across the parking area, he fished the car keys from his pocket.

He was about ten cars from the Audi when he was momentarily blinded by a white flash.

The Audi bulged from within, glass erupting everywhere. One door flew off into the air, followed by a blast of heat and then flame.

The entire car rose from the asphalt, turned once in midair, and rolled over the two cars beside it to come to rest on its side.

The shock wave hit Carter like a strong wind, sending him sprawling under the rear of a nearby car. The sound deafened him and made him lie still with his cheek against the asphalt until he passed out.

SIX

He shuffled along the dust-swirled street in perfect harmony with the other djellaba-clad herdsmen and camel drivers who moved to escape the heat of the sun. Not a single man or woman around him would guess that only twenty-four hours before he had stepped from a plane in Algiers, immaculate in a seven-hundred-dollar Savile Row suit.

Such had become his way of life for so many years. To become a chameleon and blend was to him as natural as sleeping, relieving one's body of waste, taking food, fornicating, or killing.

They were all one to him.

The village was Albebat. It was in central Tunisia, near the lake of Tozeur. He had come here many times and knew its narrow, winding streets as he knew the swiftness of his mind and hand.

At a small, open café, he turned in under the awning. His eyes, above the burnoose wrapped around the lower part of his face, shot around the rickety tables until he found a tall man dressed just like himself.

When he reached the table, the man stood almost painfully and bowed. They embraced and kissed one another on
both cheeks.

"My son, Allah is with you."

"Hassan," was all the younger man replied.

"Sit, sit, there is refreshing mint tea." They sat, and
Hassan Al-Chir stared for a long time into the other man's
eyes before he spoke again. "Ah, Ja'il, each time I see
you, you are more the man."

Ja'il Rahman nodded without responding and absently
poured himself a glass of the sweet green tea.

It was true. The frail eight-year-old-boy had truly become a man.

But he was a man with no soul. The gentle humanity he
had learned in his youth from his mother and father had
been replaced, under Hassan Al-Chir's tutelage, with a
total lack of values. While his brain was still functioning
with more than genius intelligence, his soul was vacant. He
had killed too much, too often, until it was the only passion left him.

Al-Chir and his cause had bleached from Ja'il's soul all
the value of life, his or anyone else's.

As a Palestinian commando, he had learned to kill with
expertise and without emotion or fear.

He had walked off the mountain that day so many years
before directly into the camp of Hassan Al-Chir. By showing the dagger, he was taken directly to the leader, who
greeted him warmly as the "little warrior."

Ja'il had explained that he needed a favor. He wanted
Al-Chir's approval and aid in killing his uncle.

Al-Chir had readily agreed. Abu Rahman had become a
liability anyway.

The deed was done, and Al-Chir had listened raptly as
his men relayed the gory details of the small boy as he

calmly slit his uncle's throat and then committed the ultimate desecration on the man's body.

The youth removed Abu Rahman's genitals and stuffed them in the man's mouth.

Hassan Al-Chir had listened intently, nodding now and then as the tale was told. With each word he knew that his original assessment of this fiery youth had been more than accurate.

It took only one more test.

The woman, Darva, and the two Israelis who had raided the house of Rahman were dead. But Al-Chir knew that the mind of Ja'il cried out for more revenge.

There was an Israeli army base where many Palestinians were employed. But they were carefully screened and watched. A boy like Ja'il could pull off a plan of sabotage much more easily than an adult.

For six months, the youth was carefully instructed in the fine art of making and planting bombs, then sent into Israel.

Al-Chir told him that this could be only a one-time shot. There was an Englishman, Harvey Raymond, a professor at university in Beirut. When the mission was over, Ja'il would go to Beirut as Gerald Raymond, nephew of Harvey.

The mission was devastatingly successful. The boy escaped and assumed a new identity and a new life.

But once a year, even after Harvey Raymond had retired back to England and the boy, Gerald, had been enrolled in the finest English schools, he returned to the Middle East and Hassan Al-Chir.

And there he furthered his other education, one that would make him the most feared terrorist Hassan Al-Chir controlled.

The older man at last dropped his eyes from his youthful lieutenant and spoke.

"And so, all went well?"

"As good as could be expected." Gerald Raymond related the details of Yusef Modina's death and the subsequent events.

"Excellent," Al-Chir said, nodding and sipping his tea. "The information passed on to Harvey by his little niece proved very profitable."

"Yes," the younger man replied. "Let us hope my little cousin never discovers that she was the source of her lover's betrayal and that I ended his life. I care too deeply for Ynez to lose her love and respect."

Al-Chir shrugged. "Yusef disobeyed my orders. It is his fault. I told him Ynez must be left alone. He killed himself with his treachery and disobedience. All in all you performed perfectly, as usual. It is a pity that the detonator on the bomb was defective. You would have gotten the American agent as well."

Raymond shrugged but didn't reply. Al-Chir leaned back and patted his middle. "All in all, it is a great day."

"Is it?"

"Ah, Ja'il, you have grown into such a handsome, dashing man, but so sullen. Our cause—"

"I have but one cause, Hassan: myself."

"Yes, I know," Al-Chir said, smiling crookedly. "You feed your bank accounts the same way you feed your thirst for revenge. I suppose the American's money—"

"Is safely in one of my Swiss accounts. Here is Yusef's diary."

He slid an oilskin-covered book onto Al-Chir's lap beneath the table. The older man clutched it with relief.

"Ah, Ja'il, if I had ten of you . . . no, even *two* of you . . . our cause would be won and I would be president of a new Palestine."

The younger man leaned forward, his eyes like stone.

"Hassan, old friend, you have taught me cunning, survival, and all the arts of killing. Please, do not feed me the Palestine shit you feed the others."

Al-Chir's hand came up and he ran a finger down the scar on his now beardless face. His other hand raised the glass of mint tea to his lips. All this was done with a studied calmness, but anger blazed in his dark eyes.

Raymond saw the look he knew so well, but paid it little attention. "Your other lackeys do your bidding, old friend, because their brains are soaked in piss. Please give me credit for more intelligence. The day there is a Palestinian state is the day Arafat will hunt you down and slaughter you like a dog."

Hassan Al-Chir winced. A few years ago he would have slapped the younger man's face. But no more. There was a time he could look into those cold, lifeless gray eyes and stare them down. But no more.

Hassan Al-Chir had created a monster, and in the last two years he had often shuddered at the thought of what would happen if the monster turned.

He shook his head, turned from those eyes, and threw off the mood. When he turned back he was laughing aloud. "We both must think and do what we must think and do, my son. Just remember that, even if what we think and do happens to profit us, it still puts our people closer to their homeland."

Raymond's laugh was old and tired beyond his years. "Please, Hassan, bore me no longer with this fairy tale. We know each other too well. I am a soldier; you have become a politican. I entered this war on no political stallion. I had no cause but my own survival."

Al-Chir started to object but was stopped by a look.

"I didn't lose my innocence in the warm wetness of a woman. I lost it on a bus to Amman, and you replaced it.

In Summa I lost my parents, and you moved in to fill the void."

The mint tea took on a bitter taste in Al-Chir's mouth, but he managed to stretch his lips into a smile he didn't feel. "You have become a philosopher, learning things I never taught you."

Raymond's smile mirrored Al-Chir's: it was without mirth. "You taught me well; I simply went beyond your teaching. That is why I tell you now that your war is a sham. Nothing but camel dung will follow. But it is no matter. We are both committed, and we will both continue until they finally hunt us down."

Hassan Al-Chir could only stare at his tea, as if the mint leaves could calm the nerves he had so lately acquired. *Dear Allah, how thoroughly I have schooled him. Or have I? Perhaps he was always wiser and even more bitter than I gave him credit for.*

Suddenly Raymond laughed out loud. "Come, come, old friend, don't be so glum just because I know the truth. Now, tell me, what new horrors are you hatching up for us?" He raised his glass in a mock toast.

Al-Chir strained his eyes to look beyond the young, handsome face he thought he had known so well. When he realized that he saw nothing, he sighed and began to speak.

"My colleagues in the other factions of our cause have seen fit to privately and secretly negotiate a settlement with Israel and the major powers."

"There have been negotiations before. I don't see that new ones will change anything."

"I am afraid you're wrong this time," Al-Chir growled from deep in his chest. "There have already been one-on-one individual meetings around the world for weeks. The prerequisites have been ironed out. There remains only an eye-to-eye summit to insure a treaty."

Raymond tented his finger in front of his face to mask any reaction. "Who will be in attendance?"

"Besides my *brothers* in our struggle, France, America, the USSR, Great Britain, Germany, and Israel. There will also be two representatives of the United Arab League."

Outwardly, Gerald Raymond raised only an eyebrow in reaction to Al-Chir's words. Inwardly, his stomach churned. The old warrior had reason to worry. If all these major powers were at last going to sit around the table, the very existence of Hassan Al-Chir's faction could well be nearing an end.

"Where?"

"In a castle in Luxembourg near the German border. It is called Schloss Valkyrie."

Raymond sighed, lighting his first cigarette since he had arrived. "Both the country and the castle are excellent choices. Luxembourg itself is so small that it can be sealed off easily. Schloss Valkyrie has natural defenses, as well as reinforced security set up by Hitler during the occupation."

Hassan Al-Chir again fingered his scar and leaned forward with anticipation. "That is why the challenge is so perfect for your unique talents, Ja'il. It would be your greatest coup."

"I would need help."

"Any equipment money can buy."

"And people . . . at least two, both experts."

"Han Raab has already agreed. And, of course, Leba."

Raymond nodded his assent.

Raab was a German national, the son of an executed SS officer. Besides a blind hatred of Jews, he had incredible cunning and no fear of death. He had naturally gravitated to Al-Chir's program of worldwide terrorism.

Leba Fani had been with Al-Chir since childhood. In many ways she was Ja'il's female counterpart in intelligence, guile, and training.

Ja'il's first sight of Leba Fani was still the one that always came back to him. It was when she had leaped on the front bumper of the Amman bus and, waving her rifle in the air, had shouted at the frightened occupants through the windshield.

Leba had come a long way since then, as had Ja'il. Through the years she had been Ja'il's lover as well as his friend. Leba was the only other person alive besides Al-Chir who knew about Gerald Raymond.

"It would mean exposing myself to Raab."

Al-Chir shrugged. "Kill him when his part of the operation is over."

"How much time do I have?"

"Ten days."

Raymond rubbed his eyes. *Ten days. Difficult. Almost impossible.*

He said as much.

"It is," Al-Chir agreed. "But failure will ruin us. You will do it?"

Raymond toasted again with his mint tea. "Of course I will do it, Hassan. I am too young to be forced into retirement."

And too old, he thought, *in this business to worry about dying.*

SEVEN

It was a grueling day starting at six A.M. sharp in the training facilities near Langley.

First order of business was a half hour of muscle-stretching, bone-cracking exercises under the watchful eyes of Alex Moon, the agency fitness and martial arts instructor.

"You're favoring your side, Carter."

"That's because it hurts, Moon."

"Are you saying, Carter, that a few bruised ribs from a bomb blast has put you out of commission? Bend!"

Carter bent, and then bent some more, all the while hiding the pain behind a grimace of hate directed at Alex Moon, the torturer.

"All right, that's good, Carter. Get a helmet on, and some gloves. Four three-minute rounds to check out your coordination."

Moon worked him easily at first, brushing away punches and countering with sharp jabs around the edges of his rib cage.

"You're trying to break the bruises, right, Moon?"

"No pain, no gain, Carter," the big, bullet-headed man replied, landing yet another thumping blow to the Killmaster's right side.

Carter danced away from him for the rest of that round and all of the next. Then he opened the third with a straight right that caught the other man flush on the forehead.

The blow would have felled a small tree, but all it did was make Moon smile and pain shoot up Carter's right arm.

The fourth round was a massacre. Moon moved to his head, pelting him with lefts and rights that left Carter's ears ringing.

Blissfully, it ended with Carter flat on his back but still awake.

"You're in good shape, Carter, for a beat-up old man," Moon growled, hauling Carter to his feet.

"Thanks a bunch, Moon. Now how about knives in the dark room?"

The big man roared with laughter. "No way—you're good at that! Get going, you're late for the range."

Carter checked out a Browning high-powered sniper rifle, ammo, and fifty rounds for his Luger, and hit the range.

He warmed up with simple draw-and-fire exercises at a stationary silhouette. Then he shifted to moving targets. When he felt his hand-eye coordination was smooth, he signaled a starter-timer and moved over to the range obstacle course.

"Go!" the man said, and thumbed the stopwatch in his hand.

Only two scores counted, hits and time.

Carter moved out, dead-centering a left and right target that bounced up as he ran for the scaling wall. It was six feet high and he hit it full tilt.

Over it, he lit on both feet and dropped into a crouch with the Luger back in his hands.

Two out of three moving targets, dead center, the third a shoulder hit that required a second shot for a kill.

Thirty feet ahead was the tunnel, a long section of concrete sewer pipe three feet in diameter. On either side were another pair of silhouettes. He fired twice at the one on the right, feeling the slide of his weapon lock open on the final shot, the magazine empty.

Already his left hand was digging a loaded spare from the holster on his belt. Simultaneously, he jogged the gun slightly, turning it in his grip until his thumb hit the magazine release button. The empty magazine dropped clear. The spare set in firmly. He knew it was a good change, under three seconds, and he was already firing again. Two shots into the silhouette at the left. Weapon holstered, he ran for the tunnel.

Fifteen minutes later, hands shaking with nervous energy, he was cleaning the Luger as the range master strolled over.

"You should have a bomb go off in your face more often, Nick. You bettered your last time by eleven seconds."

"Thanks a lot," Carter chuckled. "Gimme another ten minutes and I'll check out on the Browning."

"Word just came down—if you're physically up, they want you at Dupont. I'll give you a pass on the Browning. No reason you wouldn't do twenty out of twenty, since you did so well on the obstacle. What did Moon give you?"

"A green light," Carter replied, "after he beat the shit out of me."

"That's Moon," the range master said, moving away. "Don't kill anybody I wouldn't."

Carter showered, dressed, and headed for the parking

lot. Without thinking, he opened the door of his car, and then froze.

"Stop it," he hissed, slamming his butt into the bucket seat, "this is no hotel parking lot."

He drove north and hit the beltway around D.C., taking the Lee Highway cutoff. He crossed the Potomac on the Key Bridge and swung onto the Whitehurst Freeway. From there it was five minutes into the underground parking garage of Amalgamated Press and Wire Services.

The building was several floors, only two of which were used for the wire service cover. The rest of the building, including the two subbasements, were AXE headquarters.

The standard elevator deposited him in the small, businesslike first-floor lobby. He caught the security guard's eye, got a barely perceptible nod, and passed through a buzzing door into a narrower hallway that led to a second bank of elevators. These were computer controlled. Carter pushed in his personal access code and stepped inside.

But instead of pushing the button that would take him to the penthouse offices of David Hawk, he pushed "Sub-1." In seconds, the elevator descended and Carter stepped from it into the brightly lit nerve centre of AXE.

Two minutes later he was in the main computer room, approaching Damien Farrell, head of worldwide research and investigation.

"Nick, how's the side?"

"Sore as hell, thanks to Moon."

Farrell chuckled. "Thank God he can't get his hands on old bastards like me."

"Anything yet, Damien?"

"A little. Let's go into my cubbyhole where it's quiet."

Carter followed the other man into a small office with two computer consoles amid a pile of debris on a single desk. The only additional furniture were two uncomfortable chairs and filing cabinets lining all four walls.

Farrell sat and began shuffling papers, eventually handing Carter a printout. "The Spanish police has been extremely cooperative, but I'm afraid it hasn't done us much good. Here's a guest list of everyone at the Araujo villa that night, complete with background checks and interrogation results."

Carter took the thick printout and began to scan it as Farrell continued.

"All the guests, with you as the exception. check out as old friends or friends of old friends. Not all of them are lily white, but none of them fits the bill as a mad bomber."

Carter nodded. "According to this, everyone alibied everyone else for practically the whole evening, and just before the blast over half of them were in the upstairs bedrooms."

"Evidently it was that kind of a party," Farrell said wryly, picking up another sheet of paper. "Info on the blast is Gelemax, high-grade stuff."

"In other words, a little goes a long way," Carter murmured.

"You got it. Detonator was in the lid of the wine keg, just like you guessed."

Carter moved to a nearby hot plate and poured himself a cup of coffee from a standing pot. "Was it Gelemax on the Audi as well?"

"Yeah," Farrell growled, "but a different setup entirely. They found remnants of tiny aerials evidently wrapped around the explosive, as well as a Mendon high-frequency microreceiver."

Carter whirled. "That means it was visually detonated from somewhere nearby!"

"Had to be less than five hundred yards," Farrell agreed.

"Thank God for a defective detonator," Carter said, sipping from his cup.

Farrell shook his head. "No way, and I don't need a lab report from the Guardia to tell you why. The Mendon is a single-chip, solid-state baby. It operates on a pulse frequency that doesn't allow for error because of pitch. No, Nick, whoever set that baby off had you eyeballed, and did it before you got to the car on purpose."

Carter narrowed his eyes and discarded the coffee as he lit a cigarette and regained his chair. "That explains the note."

"Right. Somebody loves ya, baby."

"What about it?"

"It was printed instead of scripted, but the analysis boys came up with some bits and pieces."

"Such as . . . ?"

Farrell placed an enlarged copy of the bomber's note on the desk between them. It had chicken-scratches and inked notations on the top, bottom, and both sides.

"Ten to one it was written by an Arab. See the *i*'s and the *t*'s, the little curls? Comes from writing Arabic symbols."

Carter leaned closer. "Or Greek or Russian."

"Maybe, but pretty slim. The experts say a Semitic language. That could include Hebrew, of course. Pissed anybody off in Israel lately?"

"Probably, but I don't remember. How about personal character?"

"Damned little, mostly guesses. Bold, precise, very analytical, no nerves. Probably fastidious in dress and speech, definitely not an American or Oriental."

"That fits a few million. Could it be a woman?"

"No way."

Carter sighed, mashing out his cigarette. "Okay, we got a well-dressed Arab or Jewish bomber who loves me. What about Ja'il?"

"Nowhere, nothing. It's a fairly common Arab name, but it isn't on any list anywhere."

"What about Modina?"

"Yusef Modina, age twenty-nine. Born to wealthy parents, Damascus, Syria. Attended prep school in Paris two years, then two years at the American University in Beirut. One year unaccounted for between leaving the university and his first arrest in London."

"First arrest?"

"Suspicion, terrorist activities. Nothing proved, charges dropped."

Carter hissed through his teeth and lit up again. "Hassan Al-Chir used him for a courier. He probably had orders, once he was elevated in the organization, to stay clean. How did he get the waiter's job for the party?"

"Catering service. Two maids and a cook as well. The only full-time help that Araujo keeps in Valencia is a chauffeur and a groundskeeper. He moves around a lot from house to house."

"What else did you dig up on Ynez?"

"Ynez Khadivitt, mother Isabel, English, father Yidev, Iranian. Parents were students in Spain when they met. Both were killed in an auto accident when she was very young. Raised by the mother's brother, Harvey Raymond. He's a retired professor, lives in the Cotswolds and guest lectures on Middle Eastern affairs now and then at Cambridge."

"Raymond . . . Raymond," Carter mused, going back over the printout of the Araujo guest list. He remembered the name Gerald Raymond, and it wasn't on the list.

He closed his eyes and concentrated. He could clearly see the darkly handsome young man dancing with the overly made-up chunky woman from New York.

Her name was . . .

"Use your phone?"

"Sure," Farrell replied, and headed for the coffee.

Carter dialed Monique Leveque's number in Paris from memory. It rang several times before she picked up and answered in a breathless voice.

"Monique, Nick Carter."

"Darling, you are in Paris?"

"No, Washington."

"You are coming to Paris?"

"Not soon."

"Merde," she grumbled. "Then this is business?"

"Yeah. Remember Gerald Raymond at the villa?"

"Of course. He is gorgeous."

"The chunky little number who brought him?"

"Elvira Wertz."

"That's it," Carter said. "I've got a Guardia civil list of the guests, and neither name is on it."

Monique chuckled. "They are probably two of several not on the list. Any hint of scandal and Elvira's husband in New York would cut off her spending allowance. I imagine Vincente left her name off as a courtesy."

"Did you see them after the blast?"

"Honestly, I do not remember. I did see them just before, tiptoeing up to one of the bedrooms."

"Thanks, Monique."

"Is that it?"

"That's it. See you."

"Damn."

Carter hung up, then he scribbled both names on a pad.

"Check these two out. Specifically, find out if there's any connection between Gerald Raymond and Harvey Raymond."

"Will do," Farrell replied.

"And have the Guardia put some real pressure on Vincente Araujo. The guest lit is incomplete."

Carter left the Farrell inner sanctum and hit the private elevator to the penthouse. A guard in the outer office buzzed him through to the inner office of Ginger Bateman, David Hawk's right-hand person.

"You've been dillydallying," she chided.

"I've been playing detective in Farrell's domain. It's always nice to find out who's trying to kiss me and misses. God, you're gorgeous."

And she was, with bright blue eyes and glossy sable hair. She had sharp, striking features, and her smiling mouth was a downright erotic slash in her face. The mannishly tailored jacket and slacks did nothing to hide a knock-out figure.

"You're drooling."

"Don't I always when I come up here?"

"He's waiting."

She buzzed Carter on into Hawk's office before he could reply.

The penthouse office, in spite of windows stretching the width of one entire wall, seemed unusually dark. This, along with a constant pall of acrid cigar smoke, helped the head of AXE, David Hawk, to think.

The man himself stood behind a huge Victorian desk, glowering at papers spread before him and chewing on what Carter guessed was already the fifth cigar of the day. Under a shock of white hair were deep forehead lines that looked as if they had been etched by dragging a rake across the surface. He spoke without glancing up at Carter's approach.

"Morning, Nick, have a seat. Read this."

A stapled manila folder hit the Killmaster's lap just about the time his butt hit a high-backed leather chair.

He skimmed it quickly, then did a hard read of the last two pages marked SECURITY PRECAUTIONS.

At last he dropped it back on the desk with a heavy sigh. "Good God."

Hawk nodded. "You don't approve of the site?"

"It's okay, I suppose. I just don't know as I approve of putting all those men in one place, one room, and leaving out Hassan Al-Chir."

"I'm inclined to agree," Hawk replied, dropping his bulk into a chair and leaning back. "But the Israeli contingent, as well as our own, were adamantly opposed to recognizing Al-Chir's existence as even a negotiator."

"But by inviting him they could at least keep an eye on him."

Hawk shrugged expansively, a pained look on his face. "That would have been my preference, but politicians have their decorum to think about. How are the ribs?"

"I can go a hard ten rounds if I keep running fast enough."

"Good. I want you behind the scenes at Schloss Valkyrie."

Carter raised an eyebrow. "How far behind the scenes?"

"On the surface, check and double-check all security. Even though the meet'll be in Luxembourg, Germany is acting as host country, and Peter Reinbold, BfV, has the nod as head of security."

"Wise choice," Carter said, nodding. "I've worked with Peter. He's thorough and he doesn't make mistakes."

"You'll be unofficial backup for him from our side. That's on the surface. Underneath, I want you to nail Al-Chir or this Ja'il, whoever he is, before he puts a monkey wrench into the works."

Carter took a little time before speaking again, using some of it to light a cigarette. "With some of his own brothers there, do you really think Al-Chir will try anything?"

"I do," Hawk said with emphasis. "By agreeing to snub Al-Chir, I think the Arabs have waved a red flag in front of him. I think he'll go to any ends to prove that he's still the one to be feared. Have you updated with Farrell?"

Carter nodded. "Just a few minutes ago. Ja'il is still a total mystery. The name doesn't show up anywhere. One interesting thing . . ."

"Yeah?"

"If Ja'il is Al-Chir's alter ego, then he's probably as good or better than the old man himself. I think it was Ja'il who killed Modina at the villa. I think he was the bomber who almost got me."

"It would figure."

"But he didn't get me," Carter added. "On purpose."

He went on to explain about the remote mechanism on the bomb in the Audi. Hawk listened intently, clipping and lighting a fresh cigar. When Carter finished, he leaned forward and punched a button on his telephone console.

"Bateman."

"Yes, sir?"

"What kind of transportation do we have for Nick?"

"Military transport out of Edwards tonight at nine into Brussels."

"Thank you." He shifted back to Carter. "That gives you the afternoon. Get back down to Records and go over your old cases. If this Ja'il didn't plaster you all over the pavement, maybe he owes you one from some other meet."

"Will do," Carter said, rising. "If this Ja'il does show up, I'd like to try some kind of a scam and maybe lure Al-Chir himself out of Tripoli."

Hawk's grin was almost evil. "You have my every blessing."

EIGHT

The cottage was all charm, half-timbered and thatched roof sitting on two acres of land thick with old birch trees. Gerald Raymond parked his car on the shoulder near the gate and walked up the narrow land. Halfway, he saw her burst from the front door and sprint to meet him.

With her dark hair flying and dressed in jeans and a baggy sweater, she looked more like the little girl he had grown up with than a mature woman.

"Gerald!" she cried, and flung herself into his arms.

"Ynez, I thought you were in Spain," he lied, laughing and spinning her around and around.

"I got back a few days ago." He returned her feet to the ground and they stood facing each other. "Things didn't work out," she whispered.

"Ah, your lover jilted you." It hurt to see the pain in her eyes, but he had to say what he did to completely distance himself from any suspicion. As far as Ynez knew, he had no knowledge of Yusef Modina or their affair.

"No, not that," she replied, her cheek coming against his chest. "I don't want to talk about it."

"All right, little one. Then how about an ale for your thirsty adopted cousin?"

She brightened. "One ale coming up, and in one hour dinner with all the dishes we loved as children!"

"Where is Harvey?"

"In his study, waiting for you."

In the cottage, she ran to the refrigerator while Gerald lifted the covers from pots and sniffed with appreciation.

"Mmm, I can't wait."

"Go say hello to Uncle. I'll call you both when it's ready."

Gerald Raymond ambled from the kitchen, through the garden, and down a narrow, graveled path to the old summerhouse that had been converted into a study.

Harvey Raymond stood when the younger man slipped through the door, closing and locking it behind him.

The older man was an inch or two taller than Gerald, with broad shoulders bulkily emphasized by a heavy wool sweater. His gray hair was a tousled mop over a high, scholarly forehead and long face. Two shaggy gray brows arched above a pair of dark eyes.

"Gerald, lad."

"Harvey, it's been too long."

The two men embraced and seated themselves side by side on a huge, lumpy leather sofa.

"You saw Ynez?"

"She ran to meet me. How is she taking it?"

"Philosophically, as I have taught her to accept everything. She is better off. Meeting Modina was a bad twist of fate. She'll find another, more suitable lover, and forget the fool."

Gerald Raymond nodded in agreement. Both of these men were committed to Hassan Al-Chir and what they did. But they had both mutually agreed long before that Ynez would never know of their Palestinian connection, nor have a part of it.

Killing Yusef Modina had a twofold purpose.

"How is Hassan?"

"Getting old with creaky bones and bitterness, but still hungry."

The older man chuckled. "Tigers stay hungry until the day they die."

Gerald Raymond poured from the bottle to the glass, and perused the various papers and maps spread before them on the coffee table.

"What do you have for me?"

"Raab is in place. He has employment with a roofing firm in Trier, here, in Germany."

"Are we sure he'll be used?"

"Definitely. One of our people got to the castle weeks ago, when all this was only in the planning stages. He managed to dislodge several tiles and use an acid solution on the tar paper insulation beneath. By now there will be several leaks in the roof. Here is a plan of Schloss Valkyrie, inside and out."

The handsome young man set his glass aside and leaned closer over the table.

"All the bedrooms that will be used by the delegates are on the third floor in these two wings. Their meals will be taken here, in the large dining room. The talks will be here, in the small great room."

"Meals would be too risky," Gerald Raymond said. "Anyone with an upset stomach might miss a meal."

"Exactly. That is why our man treated only the roof directly over the conference room. Any day now, with the snow melting, the repair people in Trier will be called."

"And Leba?"

"She has rented a hunting lodge just south of St. Vith,

in Belgium. It is here, within two kilometers of the frontier. Heavy woods. It will be child's play for you to slip back and forth."

"And the materials?"

"She's working them out now in Wiesbaden. By the time you meet her tomorrow evening, everything should be ready."

"Do we have anyone inside?"

"That is being taken care of right now." Harvey Raymond checked his watch. "Probably at this very moment. The woman responsible for the food at the conference is a career employee with the Bonn government. She is also in charge of getting the castle shipshape for the meeting and its maintenance during the stay of the VIPs. Her name is Ilse Baunstaffer. She has a daughter, seventeen years old, named Therese."

Gerald Raymond nodded impassively. He didn't have to ask. Somewhere that night, in Bonn, Therese Baunstaffer would be kidnapped. Her ransom demand would not be money.

"It looks good," Gerald Raymond said. "I'll work out the details of the escape after I see the layout of the village."

"That," the older man replied, "will be the most dangerous part. Once the conference room goes up, they will seal off every road and cart path out of the country."

Gerald Raymond smiled, his eyes glazing slightly. "That is part of the challenge . . . the best part."

Static came from a small speaker near the door, followed by the voice of Ynez.

"Hey, you two, my dinner is on the table!"

"Let's eat," Harvey Raymond said, rising and rubbing his hands together. "Hungry?"

"Starved," the younger man replied with a smile. "Like a tiger."

The two men walked briskly toward the cottage and their meal, both of them easily setting aside, for the moment, the plan they were devising to murder between forty and fifty people.

Carter handed his bag up to a waiting Air Force officer, and then climbed into the big cargo jet himself.

Just before they buttoned the plane up, a dark, unmarked sedan pulled up and a man jumped out. He passed an envelope to the officer in the door and returned to the car.

Carter buckled himself in and waited for takeoff. His eyes burned. He had spent the entire afternoon going over his own reports of past missions. Nothing had jarred his memory and he found no mention of Ja'il. His memory for detail, even for events that had taken place many years before, was excellent. He trusted it. If he could not remember Ja'il, or find anything in his own reports referring to that name, there must not be a connection.

He guessed that the deliberate miss in the parking lot could only be attributed to Al-Chir's possible squeamishness about killing an American agent and stirring up more heat against him.

"Mr. Carter?"

"Yes?"

"A messenger brought this just before we took off."

Carter ripped open the envelope and scanned the five pieces of paper. *Something? Maybe,* he thought, *just maybe*.

Ynez Khadivitt and Gerald Raymond were cousins, niece and nephew of Harvey Raymond.

The background on the old professor was interesting. In fact, Carter thought, it was interesting enough to double back to England in the next day or so after checking security at Schloss Valkyrie.

"Hello."

"Good evening, mein Herr," responded the girl briskly. "May I help you?"

She was a tiny thing, standing little more than five feet tall, pretty, with short brown hair, pale skin, and eyes that slanted slightly like a cat's.

"I need some flowers for a lady."

The young girl's smile grew wider. The man didn't look much more than twenty, only three years older than she, and he was very handsome in a Latin or North African way. She also loved the way he spoke German with a little singsong effect.

"Do you see anything on display that strikes your fancy, mein Herr?"

He looked around with a puzzled frown on his face, and then back to the girl. "Not really. Is this all you have?"

"We have some of our more exotic things in the rear cooler."

"Might I have a look?"

"Of course. This way."

She held the little gate open until he passed through, and then led him into the rear of the shop.

"Are the flowers for your wife?"

"No, my mother. I'm not married."

The girl flashed him a coquettish smile. He seemed to reciprocate.

God, she thought, *he is handsome. And with Mother in Luxembourg, I can stay out as late as I want!*

"Right in here . . ."

Suddenly an arm came around her, between her breasts, the hand gripping her side and pulling her back. Another hand came over her face holding a damp cloth.

She started to scream, but no sound came. Her head was whirling and she felt as if she would vomit. She struggled, throwing her head from side to side, but he was far too strong.

When her body went limp, he laid her gently on the floor and rushed back to the front of the shop. He closed the blinds, locked the front door, and killed the lights.

She was no more than a feather in his arms as he carried her to the rear door and on into the alley. Two cars sat, their engines idling. Without being told, two men emerged from the lead sedan and lifted her.

"The bracelet, that should do it. I'll call from the frontier after I've made the contact."

The two men nodded. They wrapped the girl in blankets and placed her in the rear seat of the lead sedan. Seconds later they were driving off.

The young man climbed into the rear sedan.

"Luxembourg," he barked. "With any luck we should make it by midnight."

Ilse Baunstaffer said good night to her driver and stumbled through the gate and up the walk to the small cottage they had rented for her. She had a room at the castle, but after putting in fifteen- and sixteen-hour days, she couldn't stand to sleep there as well.

The door opened easily with her key, and she walked through the darkness of the hall into the small living room. Once there, she snapped on a lamp and went directly to the bottle she had brought with her from Bonn.

It was nearly one in the morning, but without a glass of schnapps, Ilse knew she would not be able to go to sleep.

It was the same every night. Her mind refused to shut down. Without the schnapps she would go over every room in the palace, making sure everything was clean and in its proper place. She would go over the menus and purchases for them, as well as the security of the help and each of their jobs.

Armed with the schnapps, she fell into the one comfortable chair in the room and kicked off the sensible shoes she always wore that always hurt her feet.

It was then that she saw the envelope lying on the floor in the hall. She started to rise and fetch it, but she was just too tired.

She drank her schnapps. She would open her mail in the morning.

But she didn't get her mail here at the cottage; she got it at the castle. And she had rarely received any mail anyway in the two weeks since she had arrived.

Maybe Therese . . .

The glass fell from her hand as weariness overcame her.

It was just after two in the morning when the phone rang. Automatically, her hand fumbled and found it.

"Ja, ja," she mumbled groggily.

"Frau Baunstaffer?"

"Ja, dis ist Frau Baunstaffer."

"Speak English, please."

"Yes, what is it? Who is this?"

"Have you opened the envelope?"

"Envelope? What . . ." And then she remembered and managed to focus her eyes. "No, I have not . . . what is it?"

"Get it. Open it."

She lurched into the hall, picked up the envelope, and ripped it open.

"Ach! Mein Gott!" Awake now, she ran back to the phone. "Who is this?"

"Do you recognize the bracelet?"

"Of course I do! It belongs to my daughter, Therese. I gave it to her for her last birthday. What—"

"Don't talk, Frau Baunstaffer, just listen. About four hours ago we kidnapped your daughter from the flower shop in Bonn."

"Oh, no!" the woman screamed. "Why? What do you want from me? I have no money..."

"We are not interested in money."

"What do you want?" she cried.

"Be quiet, woman, and listen! Tomorrow morning you will call the headmistress of your daughter's school and tell her that Therese has joined you for a few days. You will also call her employer in the flower shop, and inform her that Therese is ill and will not be in for a few evenings. Do you understand?"

"Yes, I understand, but why—"

"You will learn that soon. Tomorrow you will go through your day as if nothing has happened."

"How in God's name..."

"We don't care how, Frau Baunstaffer, but you will do it. No one must suspect. Tomorrow evening you will leave the castle earlier than usual. You will request a car, and drive yourself to the capital. Are you listening?"

"Of course I am listening, damn you!"

A low chuckle. "Good. A little café, La Belle Marie, on the Rue Notre Dame—it is near the Hotel Schintgen. Be there at ten sharp. You have all this?"

"I do," she managed to reply breathlessly.

"I warn you, Frau Baunstaffer, from this moment on you will be watched. If you are followed tomorrow night, one of your daughter's ears will be mailed to you the next morning."

The phone went dead, and Ilse's face went white. She

staggered to the table for more schnapps, and then back to the phone.

She dialed her apartment in Bonn and let it ring twenty times before hanging up.

Then, for a full half hour, she paced. If they didn't want money, then what did they want?

She thought she had a pretty good idea.

She got her address book from her purse and dialed Peter Reinbold's private line at the castle.

She managed to dial four of the six numbers before slamming the phone back onto its cradle.

An ear? Dear God, would they really cut off one of her baby's ears?

NINE

The Killmaster was issued an Air Force car and a Special Forces sergeant for a driver. From the look in the man's eyes and the patchwork of ribbons on his breast, Carter guessed the man might come in handy.

A little conversation on the way to the Luxembourg frontier confirmed his suspicions. Besides being a small arms and hand-to-hand expert, Ebert also knew his way around explosives.

"Just a couple of things, Sergeant."

"Yes, sir?"

"Three things. It's Nick, not sir."

"Yes—Nick."

"And get out of that uniform when we get to Valkyrie. Put on workman's clothes, whatever they wear around here."

"Okay. What else?"

"Dump this crate and get something with some piss and vinegar under the hood, even if we have to rent. I'll give you a card number."

"Gladly."

"Also, did you check to make sure everything I put on that list got into the trunk this afternoon?"

"I did," the sergeant replied with a low chuckle. "Are we planning a raid on East Berlin?"

"Not quite," Carter said, "but damned close."

Security was tight at the frontier, with Luxembourg people doing the front-end work. Neither Carter nor the sergeant missed the plainclothes people from Germany's BfV and France's SDECE massed in the background. They were like customs people at borders all over the world: sharp-eyed and stone-faced.

Even in the staff car and with Ebert in uniform, the border people went over their papers with a hard eye.

So far, so good, Carter thought when they were passed through. He spread a topographical map out on his lap.

"There's a back road up here not far to your left. Take it."

Moments later they were rising and falling through hilly, heavily forested countryside. Now and then, both to their left and right, they could see the roofs of large mansions rising through the trees.

"Pretty country," Ebert commented, gearing down to nearly a stop on the dangerous curves.

"Yeah," Carter replied, "and I'll bet at night you can't see a foot in front of your face. That turnout up ahead . . . stop there."

The sergeant parked. Carter pulled a pair of powerful glasses from his bag and they both got out.

"We walk . . . up there."

The snow was soft under their feet, making the climb precarious. They both slipped several times before reaching the top.

"Jesus," Ebert gasped, "is that it?"

"That's it," Carter said, bringing the glasses up to his face.

Schloss Valkyrie lay a mile away in the shaggy hills toward the sunset. Sitting alone across a jagged, treeless peak, it seemed to shimmer out of a Dark Ages fairy tale.

Three-foot-thick walls seemed to grow right out of the rock of the mountain, topped by crenellated battlements. Six towers soared above the walls, and through the glasses Carter could see watchful men posted at each of the old firing slits.

"It's a fortress," Ebert whispered.

"It was meant to be."

Carter shifted the glasses downward. All forestation had been removed from the base of the castle to the very foot of the mountain. There, a modern, fourteen-foot-high chain link fence had been erected. Five strands of barbed wire angled outward from the top of the fence, and Carter could see red warning signs every few feet.

"The fence is electrified and the cliffs are sheer," he said aloud. "If our boy gets in, my guess is he'll have to do it legitimately, by breaching security from the inside."

"He could steal a chopper and just blow it to hell."

"He could try," Carter replied, "if he were suicidal. But I still don't think he would get through. Look there."

He handed Ebert the glasses and pointed to a clearing in the trees about two hundred yards down from the base of the mountain.

"Gunships!"

"Four of 'em," Carter said. "And I'll bet two of them will be in the air every minute the VIPs are in there."

The Killmaster took the glasses back.

In the rear of the castle was a large lake. That was where the fence ended, but he guessed there were sensors

somewhere in the water. The only road came down the
mountain from the front of the castle, through gates, and
angled through the forest to the village of Anberg about
two miles away.

"I've seen enough," Carter said. "Let's go down to the
village and find a room. Then we'll pay our respects at the
Schloss Valkyrie."

They made their way back to the car and found three
men leaning calmly against it pointing machine pistols at
them.

"Good day, gentlemen," said the tallest of the three.
"Could we see your papers, please?"

Carter smiled as he handed the man his identification.
Peter Reinbold wasn't taking any chances.

Gerald Raymond stepped from the train to the platform
in Wiesbaden and made directly for the exit doors of the
station.

He was dressed as a laborer, in heavy trousers and a
checkered shirt beneath a bulky winter coat. He carried no
bag, and wore a multicolored woolen cap pulled low over
his forehead and ears.

He walked through the lightly falling snow at a steady
but unhurried pace toward the Rhine. Once at the river, he
paused for a few seconds, got his bearings, and bore to the
right. Nearly a mile from the center of the city, he left the
river and moved into a residential section of large, old
homes that had been chopped up into apartments.

The house he headed for was gray stone with light blue
shutters long since faded. He bypassed the front entrance
and walked down a narrow, cobbled path to the rear. Steps
and an iron railing led down to a basement apartment.

His knock brought movement at the curtained window,
and the door opened at once. Raymond stepped inside, the

door closed behind him, and Leba Fani moved into his arms.

The kiss was almost perfunctory, with passion but muted with the mutual knowledge that sex would come later, after business had been completed. This knowledge was at the core of their relationship.

"Any trouble?" Leba asked when the kiss ended.

"None," Raymond replied, shrugging off his coat. "A fishing boat across the Channel, a train across Belgium to the German frontier where I walked across, then another train here. Should anything go wrong, I'm in the Cotswolds sipping sherry with my uncle or recuperating from a bad cold in my London flat."

She brushed her lips over his cheek. "It is good to be working again. Drink?"

"Please. Whiskey."

"We're terrible Muslims," she chuckled.

"I know."

Raymond watched her body move across the room in a clinging dark blue robe. A model or a movie star of the same height might have weighed ten pounds less, but Leba was not at all heavy for the broad, full design of her body. And Raymond knew all too well what she could do with that body. She was more than a match for any man with the deadly speed of a cobra.

"To success," she toasted, handing him one of the two glasses.

"And survival afterward," he murmured, eyeing her over the rim of the glass.

Her two most striking features were the wide, deep green eyes, ingenuous yet provocative, and the prominent cheekbones that gave her beauty an almost feline, sinister quality. The wild mane of hair, down now, was an unqualified black. Her legs and arms were strong and graceful, her hips properly parabolic, her breasts high.

All in all, Raymond thought, he would probably be her lover even if he were not her coworker. Besides, the idea that she was fully capable of turning on him at any time—and killing him—gave an interesting fascination to the relationship.

"You are thinking about my body rather than my mind," she teased.

Raymond smiled. "I take your mind for granted. How far along are we?"

"The car, a four-door Renault, nearly new. It was stolen four weeks ago in Geneva, and the engine and papers were worked over in Paris. It's in the parking lot at the rear. I rented the hunting lodge in St. Vith as a blonde. We'll be newlyweds, with the name you'll be using as a workman."

"Good. And the materials?"

"In the bedroom, this way."

In the apartment's only other room, he helped her move the bed aside. This done, she used a crowbar to lift four wide planks from the floor. Together they withdrew too fat bundles wrapped in leather thongs.

Inside the blankets were two Uzi submachine guns, each packed with two hundred rounds of ammunition already in magazines. The only other arms were three Heckler and Koch VP70 machine pistols, also with several extra magazines.

"Silencers?"

"Still in the cartons, there."

Raymond nodded. "None of this is traceable?"

"All stolen over a year ago from the depot near Frankfurt."

Next he removed a plastic box and opened the lid. Inside were twenty eight-ounce, paper-wrapped cartridges of Gelemax.

"I prefer Quarrex," the woman said.

"Too unstable for this job. Gelemax can be molded more easily with the hands and retains its shape better. Also, it doesn't react to heat or cold. What about the electronics?"

"Two transmitters, two receivers, the detonator, a dozen transistor batteries, and the aerials." She counted all these items on her fingers. "They are already at the lodge."

Raymond smiled. "You're as thorough as ever, my darling," he said, rewrapping everything and replacing the bundles in the floor space. "I assume the car has been rigged?"

Leba nodded. "Added sections of the gas tank and the frame . . . plastic, but oil- and dirt-stained. I checked; it's impossible to detect."

Back in the large living room, Raymond poured himself another drink. "You've made contact for my papers?"

"I called on the union hall here in Wiesbaden this morning and made contact with Herr Ernst Bachmann. He assured me that they have several thatching experts who can repair our villa."

Raymond leaned back in his chair, closing his eyes with a satisfied sigh. "You have done well, Leba, as always. What about Raab?"

"He is difficult to work with at times. Hatred clouds his brain. But he has done his part thus far. He has five surface-to-air Sidewinders, and he has been checked out on the launcher. And he had no trouble getting employment at the roofing company in Trier." She paused, smiling. "It seems two of their best men had a serious automobile accident last week and they are shorthanded."

"Then all we need is the makeup job on me in the morning to get my working papers, and we are go."

Raymond opened his eyes and smiled.

Leba had stood and discarded the robe. Now she stood directly in front of him, completely nude.

"Now that you are satisfied about business, I think we should relax."

As she removed his clothing, Raymond let the supple beauty of her body inflame the passion in his.

Naked, her athletic body was even more erotic than he remembered it. There were no blemishes or scars, no unsightly sags. The rounded fullness of her breasts was marred by only the sightest suggestion of veins. The lush mounds were capped by aureoles that were wide and very dark. They swelled under the ministrations of his hands.

"Do you still let Hassan make love to you?"

"Now and then," she replied without emotion.

"Is it good . . . with him?"

"It is functional. Why do you ask? Don't tell me there is jealousy as well as ice in your veins, Gerald."

"No, just curiosity," he lied.

He did feel jealousy for the first time. Why? Was he getting weak, beginning to care?

He had failed to kill Carter when he knew it was the best thing to do. Now he suddenly wanted to possess Leba instead of just using her.

The thought of experiencing any genuine emotion frightened him. He considered it a sign of weakness, and weakness meant failure, or, worse yet, death.

He buried it by concentrating on her body, taking her right breast between his fingers. With a gentle laziness he shook it back and forth, and at the same time lowered his lips and teeth to the nipple.

"Harder," she gasped. "You know what I like!"

Raymond responded to her remark by increasing the action of his tongue and teeth on her rigid nipple. At the same time, his fingers cruelly squeezed her pliant breast.

She responded with a groan of pain filled with desire. It worked, erasing the previous emotion he had felt, leaving nothing but the purely physical desire of a male body for one that is female.

Leba released a tortured moan and her fingers worked in his hair. As he continued punishing her with his hand, he brought his mouth to her lips. He toyed with her tongue, then chased it back into her mouth.

Suddenly she closed her teeth tightly against his tongue and tensed the tip with the rubbing rotation of her own. At the same time she dug her nails viciously into his back and slammed her body against him.

Passion surged through Raymond, demanding its release. He pushed her down to the floor and fell with her, moving his hands upward over the inner part of her agitated thighs. They yielded at once. He positioned himself and fell forward on his elbows, running his hands beneath her body and downward to clasp her tensed buttocks.

"Yes, now...hurt me with it, Ja'il!" The words emerged like a growl from her chest.

Lifting her slightly, he pressed forward and shifted until he found her. She twisted, but he held back, maintaining only external contact.

"Don't tease, damn you!" she hissed.

When he persisted, her hand arced through the air, the sound of her palm on his cheek like the crack of a rifle.

Only then did he plunge into her, moving her a full foot on the carpet.

She cried out and her feet left the floor. He felt her heels skinning up his thighs to pound his back.

"Yes!" she screamed. "Hurt me with your need, Ja'il!"

Her legs almost strangled him in her need, and Raymond squeezed her buttocks and began giving of himself in avid concentration, letting his hips go their own way...

thrusting, rolling, rocking from side to side.

"Yes, yes! I love it, Ja'il!" she moaned as she responded to each motion with a countermotion of her own.

As their tempo gradually increased, he released her buttocks and moved his hands high beneath her to clasp her upper body against him. Her anxious hips began to pound in trip-hammer fashion, not satisfied with what they were getting, wanting more and wanting it faster.

He responded, cruelly driving up the steep slope of passion with short avid thrusts, each one taking him just that much closer to the top. He worked against a tremendous pressure that was closing in on him . . . engulfing him . . . thickening . . . swamping his senses . . . letting him know and feel nothing except the throbbing need of his desire as it struggled for release.

He could feel Leba nearing the top also. Her mouth was open, her head tossing from side to side. She was making low incoherent sounds, which then changed to a higher-pitched series of soft little cries. She had lost all semblance of restraint now and her lithe body was hammering up at him.

Raymond thrust wildly, and suddenly the woman tightened and seemed to hang in suspension. She cried out just as he clawed at the pinnacle, tumbled over it, and plunged downward into a chasm. Released, he fell across her perspiring body.

"Animals," he gasped. "We're animals."

"No, we are human," Leba replied vacantly. "Animals eat the flesh they kill."

TEN

The snow had begun during the early evening, before she had left the castle. Now, three hours later, it rained down in huge white fluffs, dancing crazily in the channels of wind in front of the car.

Ilse Baunstaffer, her knuckles white on the steering wheel, made several wrong turns before she found the Rue Notre Dame. It was one of the oldest streets in Luxembourg's tiny capital, beginning at the rail station and ending several blocks away at the cathedral of the same name.

When she saw the vertical, faintly lit sign of the Hotel Schintgen, she pulled to the curb and parked.

It was five minutes before ten, but she didn't get out of the car. She had to gather her thoughts, put her analytical Germanic mind in order.

Ilse had not smoked in three years. She had started smoking again that morning. Peter Reinbold, head of security at the castle, had noticed.

"You look worn out, Ilse. Why don't you take the day off? We have time."

She had declined, but the look he had given her had sent chills of fear up her spine.

No one must suspect, the voice on the phone had said. *Go through your day as if nothing has happened.*

Good God, Ilse thought, *how can I act natural?*

She mashed out her cigarette and narrowed her red-rimmed eyes, searching for a sign. The headlights of passing vehicles reflected dully off the wet pavement, while streetlights glowed ineffectively like old gas lamps through the falling snow.

The snow is melting as fast as it falls. The leak in the roof over the conference room will be even worse by tomorrow. She would have to call the roofing people in Trier back in the morning.

And the linen for the bedrooms was a mess. It would have to be redone.

"Damn," Ilse suddenly cried aloud, and struck the steering wheel. And again cursed herself silently.

Her daughter's life was in danger and she was thinking about her job.

And then she saw the faint, flickering sign, several doors beyond the hotel and across the street: La Belle Marie.

Forcing herself to move, Ilse pulled up the collar of her coat and stepped from the car. With each step she felt that there were a million eyes watching her.

Two doors from the entrance to the café, she was halted abruptly by a voice coming from a darkened doorway.

"You have done well so far, Frau Baunstaffer. See that you continue."

She started to whirl toward the doorway.

"Do not turn and do not speak. Continue on up the street to the cathedral. Go inside. Light a candle at the altar, and exit by the side door. That is all. Now, walk."

The next minutes passed in a snowy haze. Ilse managed to light the candle, and even took time for a brief prayer.

Just as she stepped from the alcove to the street, a small dark sedan slid to a halt in front of her. The rear door opened and a figure emerged from the shadows behind her. Powerful hands propelled her into the car, onto the floorboards.

She started to scream, but it was cut off when some kind of a bag was thrust over her head, and the car lurched forward.

"Don't do anything but breathe, woman. It will not be long."

Ilse thought it was the same voice from the doorway. For the next fifteen minutes she lay like a stone with two pairs of heavy feet holding her down.

The car had barely come to a halt when she was dragged from it. A door opened and she was half dragged, half carried up a flight of steps. Then she heard another door opening, and she was slammed into a chair and the hood removed.

She was seated at a desk, a high-intensity lamp in front of it shining directly into her eyes. Beyond the lamp she could make out the shape of two or three men, but no faces.

"You are a wise woman, Frau Baunstaffer." It was the voice she had heard the previous evening on the telephone. "There are four Polaroid photographs on the desk before you. Examine them, please."

Ilse looked down and gasped. All four photos were of her daughter Therese. One by one she picked them up with a shaky hand. The first and second were close-ups of her daughter's elfin, frightened face. The third showed Therese sitting upright on a bed, her hands bound tightly together and a blindfold across her eyes.

Unconsciously, Ilse's habitual compulsiveness took in every detail of her daughter's clothing and the room. It was a woman's room, with fresh flowers in a vase along with a telephone on a bedside stand. There was also a radio on the stand. The bed was oak spool with a white spread. Near the bed was a chest of drawers with an oval mirror over it. A brightly colored fabric runner covered the top of the chest. In the mirror she could see two windows with white lace curtains.

"Please hurry, Frau Baunstaffer . . . the fourth picture."

This one did bring a tiny scream from Ilse's throat. It was a close-up of the side of Therese's head with the hair pulled back. There were two male hands in the picture, one holding the top of her daughter's ear away from her head. In the other hand was a straight razor.

"Good God, what do you want?" she gasped.

"Not much. Just some cooperation. If we get it, your daughter will be returned to you without being harmed."

"What are you going to do?"

The man ignored the question. "Did you make the telephone calls as we instructed?"

"Yes."

"Good. Do you know the firm of Feltner and Sons, furniture refinishers in Leuven?"

Ilse wracked her troubled brain, but she couldn't recall the name. "No . . . why?"

"The table in the conference room at the castle is an eighteenth-century Fineburg, is it not?"

Ilse's features mirrored her jumbled mind. "Yes, it's an antique of the region made by August Fineburg in 1752."

"There are six legs on the table. Two on one side were weakened some time ago when the table was moved from the great hall. Correct?"

"Yes." How, she thought, could they know all this?

"Also, because of clumsy movers, there were several small scratches on the two legs, as well as on the top."

"Yes, that is so."

"Tomorrow morning, Frau Baunstaffer, you will call Feltner and Sons to pick up and repair the table."

"I can't do that. I've already discussed the table with the castle's custodian, and we both agreed that there was no need to repair the table. He himself put a brace on the legs."

"No matter," the dry, disinterested voice continued. "You will send the table out for repairs."

"I can't, damn you!" Ilse cried.

"You are in charge, Frau Baunstaffer. You can do anything you want to do."

"I cannot! Besides, this company, Feltner and Sons, isn't on our approved list."

"Then put them on the approved list!" the voice barked.

Suddenly a gloved hand reached forward into the light and turned on a portable cassette player she had not noticed.

"Mutti, I am all right now, but they say . . . they told me the most awful things they would do to me . . . Mutti, there's a man with a razor, he said he would send pieces of me—"

"Stop! Stop it!" Ilse screamed, covering her ears with her hands.

The tape was killed.

"Tomorrow morning, Frau Baunstaffer, you will make the call. And you will tell no one of this. Believe me, we have ways of knowing. If you do, we will kill your daughter, and, I assure you, the body will never be recovered."

The voice was cold, a monotone, and the words were said with such calm conviction that Ilse was sure every word was meant.

The light woolen dress she wore beneath her raincoat was soaked with perspiration and her eyes had become glazed with fear.

"Well, Frau Baunstaffer, what is your decision?"

"What are you going to do, put a bomb in the table?"

"You don't really want to know."

Ilse put her arms on the table and dropped her head to them. For twenty years she had been like a rock, devoted to duty. Her whole being had, over the years, been trained to obedience and loyalty. What this man was asking her to do went against all her strong moral fiber.

"I don't have all night, Frau Baunstaffer."

"Yes . . . yes, I'll do it."

"Take her back to her car."

The lake was shimmering black in the mist beginning three hundred yards before them and ending a quarter of a mile beyond in the jagged rocks at the base of the hill.

"See 'em?" Carter asked.

Sergeant Tom Ebert nodded as he lowered the night glasses from his eyes. "There are two. One's moving along the edge of the lake, there. He does half a perimeter and comes back. The other one's in that thicket, about forty yards back from the lake. I'd say he's working a sound sensor from the way he's been moving."

"They in contact?"

"Yeah," Ebert replied, "every few minutes with walkies. Also, Nick, I'd say there's a third one somewhere as a backup. He probably doesn't show unless they flush something."

Carter smiled and gently patted the top of a cage at his feet. "That's why we have ol' Sly here."

From behind the wire mesh of the cage, the bright eyes

of a small red fox stared dolefully out at the two men.

"I'll take the left flank and nail him when he shows himself," Carter said. "You move in as soon as the control man zeroes in on Sly. Give me a count of fifty."

Ebert's darkened face nodded, and Carter moved off silently, being careful to stay outside the effective range of the sound sensor.

Both men wore dull black wet suits with hoods. Their only weapons were West German-manufactured Magnar stun guns, effective up to about twenty-five feet. Tied to the backs of their utility belts were hard-soled oilskin boots, hard rubber cleats attached to the soles. The last piece of equipment was the most necessary: a pair of hard rubber claws that could be attached to the wrist and would extend out over the hands and fingers. The fingers of the claws were long and sharp, and when used properly, acted exactly like the front paws of a cat.

Under his breath, Carter was counting. When he reached fifty he stopped and brought his own night glasses into play.

He barely heard the rustling sound to his rear and right, but through the glasses he saw the control man's head come up alertly. A split second later he brought a walkie up to his mouth.

Beyond the contact man, Carter saw the sentry at the lake take off. With any luck he would spot the fox and drop his guard long enough for Ebert to nail him.

Sound to his left made Carter whirl the glasses in that direction. Ebert had been right. He was just in time to see a sentry in full camouflage gear drop out of a tree and head in the direction given him by the sensor control man.

Carter dropped to his belly and moved forward on a line that would intersect. He did, twenty seconds later, and dropped the man like a tree with the stun gun.

He had scarcely hit the ground before the Killmaster was on him. He strapped the sentry's helmet under his chin and took the battery pack and earphone. As he moved forward, he put the pack in his belt and the plug in his ear.

It was only a receive unit, so he wouldn't have to reply to the control man.

"Kohl, you're heading right for it. Hans, go left . . . no, left, you fool! You're heading right for me!"

Seconds later, Carter was five feet from him, and stood up.

The control man swiveled his head around. "Hans, damn you . . ."

The helmet fooled him for only a few beats, but it was long enough. Before he could unshoulder his machine pistol, Ebert lunged up behind him like a detached shadow and engufled his face with two big hands.

It took about two breaths and he was out. When the man was limp, Ebert lowered him gently to the ground. He tossed the soaked pad away and placed the man's helmet under his head like a pillow.

"How much did you give him?" Carter whispered.

"Enough for major surgery," Ebert replied, already moving toward the lake with Carter close behind.

They went into the water side by side, and breaststroked across. A low stone wall ran along the water's edge. They stopped just short of it, and both of them took small, battery-powered pulseometers from under their suits. Carter squinted at the jumping needle and looked up at the top of the wall.

"There . . ."

"And there," Ebert said. "About four feet apart, going two ways."

They walked directly to the wall and raised their hands, poising the small instruments together.

"Ready?" Ebert nodded. "Now!"

As one, they set the pulsers down on top of the wall and anxiously watched as the needles kept up their rhythmic jumping as they intercepted and reflected the silent pulsations from the other two already on the wall.

One at a time they scrambled over. When the boots and claws were in place, they started up. Though the rock face was sheer to the eye, up close there were edges and even holes of erosion caused by centuries of weather. The climbing was much easier than they had expected. It took just less than a half hour to reach the upper wall.

Again, a pulser was used to check for sensors. When none was found, they began to work their way around to the side below the conference room.

"There may be dogs," Ebert hissed.

"I'm sure there are," Carter whispered, "but more than likely they're kept just for sniffing out explosives. When they're not being used, they're probably kept in the courtyard on the other side. Up you go!"

Carter boosted Ebert to his shoulders. The sergeant was able to get a good grasp on the top of the wall. When he did, Carter crawled right up his legs and over his body. When he was flat out on top, he helped Ebert up.

Head to head, they lay on top of the wall. Below them was a small courtyard. On the inner side were steps leading up to the next level, one below their objective.

Silently, they dropped into the courtyard and padded across. Just short of the steps they paused to unscrew the rubber cleats. This done, they tied the claws back to their belts and continued.

An iron gate, padlocked, barred them at the top. It took

fifteen seconds for Carter to pick it.

They were in the walkway directly below the conference room. The wall up was made of uneven stone. Between where they stood and the base of the windows was about forty feet and two ledges.

It was the easiest part.

Again, Carter used the pulse detector.

Nothing.

They started up, and just as they hit the first ledge Carter knew it was all over.

There were over a hundred roosting pigeons. Half of them were frightened into flight, and the other half raised a din that could be heard a mile away.

Spotlights came on from both nearby towers, illuminating the entire wall and the two human flies clinging to it.

It wasn't five seconds until the walkway below them was filled with armed men. The windows above them opened and more machine pistols pointed down at them.

"Climb down slowly! Let me warn you, any offensive move and you will be shot!"

"Goddamned pigeons," Carter muttered. "The oldest alarm system in the world."

Ebert chuckled. "So much for high-tech terrorism."

By the time they reached the walkway, a beetle-browed, cigar-chomping Peter Reinbold, in a bathrobe, was awaiting them.

"You are both under arrest! Take them—"

"Good evening, Peter," Carter said, pulling the hood from his head. "Charming little place you've got here."

"Carter . . . Nick Carter!" the man replied in English. "What the hell . . . ?"

"Let me say, Peter, that your night security is impeccable. If your daytime watch is as good, we should be home free."

The tall German smiled. "I should have guessed when you didn't check in with me earlier this evening."

"Well, now that I have, the least you can do for the sergeant and me is buy us a beer."

ELEVEN

Gerald Raymond awakened early to the business of the day. He made coffee and a light breakfast for the two of them. When they had finished, Raymond showered and very carefully shaved. This done, he returned to the bedroom and, naked, sat before a lighted mirror.

Leba Fani had already laid out her materials on the dresser. Across the room, a sheet had been stretched across the wall, and in front of it two lights and a large press camera on a tripod had been set up.

For the next hour, she worked with deliberate patience on Raymond's face. Using a mixture of spirit gum and latex, she aged his forehead, his cheeks, and the skin of his neck. Plastic tubes gave his nostrils an aristocratic flare and also thickened his nose. Carefully, using just a touch of makeup on her thumb, she worked graying shadows into the latex as it set.

"You are a genius, Leba."

"I've done it enough times on myself," she replied, chuckling low in her throat. "Now the hair."

Using clippers and comb, she restyled his curly hair. A

light application of mousse and a dryer removed the curl enough so it could be combed straight back, giving even more severity to the aged face. Meticulously, she combed gray into the temples until only a hairdresser at very close range could detect that it wasn't natural.

The previously made mustache also contained light flecks of gray. With the proper addition of makeup around the edges of the pantyhose material to which the mustache had been spirit-gummed, it, too, was impossible to detect.

At last Leba stood back. *"Voilà* Herr Whoever-you're-going-to-be."

"Is the camera ready?"

"I'll load it while you dress."

Raymond put on a workingman's heavy blue shirt, a rather ragged tie, and a cap. By the time he was dressed, Leba had loaded the camera and focused the lights.

She took four shots, two side and two frontal views.

"I'll have these developed by the time you get back."

Raymond undressed and dressed again in a conservative, dark blue pin-striped suit, white-on-white shirt, and dark tie. The suit had been especially tailored and padded to add several pounds where a man of his new age would have pounds.

"I should be back in not more than two hours."

Leba only nodded. She was already at work.

Raymond walked the eight blocks to the Guild Hall and arrived at precisely nine, the moment the doors were being opened.

"My name is Nathan, John Nathan. I believe my wife spoke to a Herr Bachmann yesterday about a workman for our villa in Luxembourg."

"Ja, Herr Nathan," the young woman replied. "Please go right in there. Herr Bachmann is expecting you."

The guildmaster was a paunchy little man with specta-

cles, a jovial, wheezy manner, and a red face. He jumped
to attention the moment Raymond stepped into the office.

"Your wife mentioned that you wished the fellow to be a
journeyman roofer, and that the work would be in Luxembourg."

"That is correct," Raymond replied. "About three
months, I expect."

"Good, very good. I think I have just the man for you. I
have brought three in for you to interview. Of course, to
work in Luxembourg, he will have to acquire a permit for
foreign labor if he doesn't already have one. That will be
between the two of you."

"I understand."

"But I do have the forms right here."

He passed two forms across the desk. Raymond folded
and pocketed them. Bachmann leaned his thumb on the
console button in front of him. He kept it there until the
door opened and the young secretary stepped in.

"Have the three roofers come in yet?"

"*Ja, mein Herr.* They are all here."

"Would you show Herr Nathan the way to the hall,
please?"

"*Ja, mein Herr.* This way, please."

Raymond followed the woman into a huge room fes-
tooned with slogans and No Smoking signs. There were
long benches down the middle and cubicles along the
walls.

"Right there, *Herr Nathan,*" she said. "Those are the
three men Herr Bachmann has called in."

Raymond scrutinized each of them carefully. One was
barely five foot three and far too young, even if he had a
decided bald spot right on the top of his head. He would
never do.

"I'll interview the middle one first."

She crooked a finger, and the middle man trotted over to follow Raymond into one of the cubicles.

"Good morning," Raymond said. "Do you speak English?"

"*Ja*. My name is Gortmann."

"The work will be steady for three months, with good pay and transportation back here every weekend."

"Abroad, eh?"

"Luxembourg."

"Oh." The man's hand dived into his jacket and withdrew a large piece of official-looking paper. Proudly, he displayed it.

"I have working papers for Luxembourg."

Then, Raymond thought, *you will never do*.

He went through the small, youngish man with cursory questions, and then motioned in the third.

He was about the right size and weight, and was definitely the right age, with dark hair and smoky gray eyes.

Beneath the desk, Raymond crossed his fingers and asked the question.

"No, sir, I have never worked outside of Germany."

"How does the sound of it hit you?"

"Fine, sir. My wife and I have had it hard lately. We could use the money." His voice was eager.

"Can you leave in a few days' time?"

"Oh, yes, sir."

"And what is your name?"

"Freehof, sir. Ludwig Freehof."

Raymond studied him. The man was the right height and the eyes were perfect. Also, he had no tattoos on his hands or arms, and no scars or distinguishing marks.

"You'll do," Raymond said. "I'll tell Herr Bachmann it's settled. You do have a copy of your work record sheet?"

"Yes, sir, right here."

As they walked back toward the guildmaster's office, Raymond asked offhandedly, "You do know you'll have to get a Luxembourg work permit?"

"Yes, sir. I'll qualify, sir; my sheet's good."

"I'm sure it is. And you'll have to have your birth certificate . . ."

"It's at home. I can get it in an hour, sir."

"Excellent. While I'm in here, get a couple of pictures of yourself at the Rapid Photo booth there in the hall."

The man scurried away, and Raymond reentered Ernst Bachmann's office. It took only a few minutes to sign the forms and get Bachmann's assurance that he would send the notice of employment to the Labor Commission within the hour.

He picked up Freehof in the lobby and guided him across the street to a bar. At a table, they ordered and Raymond took out the two application forms.

"I'll give you a hand filling these out."

The man wrote, tongue-guiding his pen, giving age, birthplace, and description.

"No, no, don't sign it. We both have to sign it in front of a notary solicitor."

Raymond paid, and they walked two blocks to a solicitor's office he had spotted earlier.

The man barely glanced at the forms and both men's driving permits and passports. Even if he had looked closely at Raymond's he wouldn't have realized that they had been manufactured in the basement of a hotel in Tripoli, Libya.

"Well now, that was easy, wasn't it?" Raymond said with a smile as they exited the solicitor's office.

"Yes, sir."

"Why don't I just walk along with you and pick up your birth certificate? I'll take care of the rest of this myself this afternoon."

The man was more than happy to oblige.

Raymond followed him across the city. The farther they walked, the more the area deteriorated. Small, dimly lit stores, many of them dusty basement shops, interlaced with old stoops in front of run-down residences. Eventually they entered an even shabbier tenement section.

Buildings, separated by entrances to pitch-black alleys, were crumbling. Raymond saw soggy heaps of debris and dented, overflowing garbage cans in the alleys.

Freehof saw the look on Raymond's face. "As I said, sir, we've fallen a little on hard times."

He opened the door with a key, and a thin, sallow-faced woman met them. The news that her husband had found employment did little more than bring tears to her weary eyes, but she did manage to thank Raymond in broken English.

"I'll get the birth certificate."

Freehof left the room, and Raymond was left awkwardly with the wife.

The woman looked sick, skinny to the point of emaciation, all elbows and shins. Her skin had a waxy, translucent look. She wore rimless glasses, and the plain dark dress looked like a tent on her frail body.

"Here we are. I'd forgotten where it was for the moment."

Raymond took the birth certificate and pressed a sheaf of bills into the other man's hand.

"I'll be back to you day after tomorrow. In the meantime, there's a little advance."

Quickly, Raymond exited before the man could count

the money and begin to wonder why he deserved a full month's pay before he even started work.

True to her word, Leba had the photographs ready when he returned to the apartment. "You found one?"

"Yes, he's perfect," he snorted.

"You don't have to take my head off."

"Sorry."

Without saying anything else, Raymond changed into the workingman's outfit and left again at once.

At the labor office, he paused to study a set of regulations he knew by heart: Only under exceptional circumstances would foreign stamped work permits be issued before the prescribed time.

Inside the door of the main entrance, a young woman sitting behind a switchboard was handling telephone calls and greeting visitors. The churlish look on her plain face and the abruptness with which she pulled out and plugged in the spaghettilike cords clearly demonstrated a disaffection for the role. But there was little in her manner or appearance to suggest that the switchboard would have much competition for her attention.

"Could you help me, please? I've got a job in Luxembourg and I need work papers and a foreign stamp."

"It's not on this floor," the girl answered sourly.

Raymond resisted the temptation to shove a handful of the wires down her throat. "Well, can you tell me where I have to go?"

"Renewal or first application?"

"First application."

"Trades or domestic?"

"Trades. I'm a roofer."

"Third floor, room three-twelve," she answered, yawning in his face.

Raymond carried his cap in his hand into 312. "My name is Ludwig Freehof," he said to the bored man behind the counter. "I think Herr Bachmann at the Guild Hall sent over a notification of employment for me."

The man nodded, his pale blue eyes impassive. "Papers."

Raymond laid the two applications on the desk along with Freehof's birth certificate.

"Pictures."

He laid out the four photographs Leba had taken of him earlier.

"It says here you start work tomorrow," the man mused. "That's very short notice."

"I know, sir. I need the job very badly. I've been unemployed for almost a year."

The man nodded and flipped the pictures over. "You didn't sign the photographs."

Raymond's gut froze, but his inner turmoil didn't show as he picked up the pen with a steady hand and managed to maneuver the signed application form to a place right beside the photos.

The scrawl was a childish one, easily duplicated with a wavering hand.

You're slipping, Ja'il. Damn, but you're slipping.

The man gathered up the photos and the papers and disappeared through a door behind him.

Raymond sat down and lit a cigarette. He knew the procedure. Somewhere behind that partition there was a looker, a man who did nothing all day long but look at photographs on applications. He would blow them up on a screen and compare them with mug shots from police departments all over Germany, as well as mug shots of known terrorists from the BfV.

At least on that score Raymond felt safe. The only pictures in existence of the face he was wearing were the ones he had just given the clerk.

He looked up as the man reentered the room and sent a flurry of stamps across the papers.

"Pay your fee in room nine, basement. There will also be a small rush charge."

With his cap still in hand, Raymond went down to the basement, handed over the materials, and paid the fee.

"Three o'clock."

"Pardon?"

"Your papers . . . they will be ready at three o'clock."

"Thank you."

Raymond walked to a corner bar, cursing himself every step of the way. *Slipping, you're slipping. What else have you forgotten?*

He had lunch standing at the bar. Suddenly he pushed the beer away and ordered a whiskey. It was hot in the heavy jacket and shirt.

Or was he just sweating?

He ate the rest of his meal with an effort, recognizing the necessity of eating. He forced down potatoes that were too floury, meat whose flavor had been left in the pan, and vegetables that weren't cooked. He managed to finish the whiskey, thankful that it took the edge off his anger toward himself.

There was still an hour to kill.

He bought a pad and envelope at a nearby store, and wandered into a park. On a bench, he scrawled a note of apology to Ludwig Freehof, telling the man that he wouldn't need him after all.

Then he put the note, the birth certificate, and some bills—for any inconvenience—into the envelope and mailed it on his way back to the Labor Commission.

His papers were ready.

As he walked back to the apartment in the brisk after-noon air, he knew there was no doubt of it.

He *was* sweating.

TWELVE

Carter didn't know what to expect, so he was only mildly surprised at Ynez Khadivitt's warm reception when he stepped from the car.

"Some business in Portsmouth," he explained. "Thought I would just stop by on my way back to London."

"I'm glad, so glad you did."

She linked her arm through his and guided him into the cottage. Carter watched her face, her eyes, to see any change in her expression. She had never told him her uncle's address in England, so it would be natural for her to wonder how he had found her.

She didn't. The open innocence never left her eyes, nor the smile her lips.

Ynez sat him down in the kitchen and immediately went about making tea.

"How is everything?"

"You mean my mental condition?" she replied.

"Yes, I guess I do."

"Fine, really. Uncle has helped me understand. Yusef

was involved in something he couldn't escape. It's all for the best, really. Our lives would have been awful. Cream . . . lemon?"

"Neither," Carter said. "Is your uncle here? I'd like to meet him."

"No, this is his lecture night. He won't be back until late this evening. He'll be sorry he missed you. I've told him about you . . . in Spain."

"Have you?" Carter masked his face with his cup and mentally prepared himself to cover her reaction to the next question. "And your cousin, is he here?"

"Gerald? No, he was for a day, but he returned to London. He wasn't feeling well, and he said he was just going to hibernate in his flat rather than give us whatever he'd caught."

They chattered through a second cup of tea before the perplexed frown he had expected appeared.

"You know Gerald?"

"Yes, I met him at a couple of parties. He mentioned Cambridge and the American University in Beirut. That, and the name, put it all together."

She nodded and the frown disappeared. Carter breathed a silent sound of relief. Everything might be coincidence, but he had learned through the years that too much coincidence could breed interesting connections.

"It was Gerald, actually, who introduced me to Yusef originally. Needless to say, he feels very badly about it now."

"Yes," Carter agreed, "I suppose he does. Ynez, tell you what . . . why don't you pop over to London with me tonight? We'll take in a show and dinner. You can stay with Gerald, and train back in the morning."

Her face was like a two-hundred-watt bulb coming on. "Oh, that would be grand! It is getting a little boring here.

Uncle spends nearly all his time in his study."

"Then let's do it. You change and pack an overnight bag."

She bounded up, kissed him on the cheek, and was gone.

The main floor of the cottage was small. Coming through it to the kitchen, he had seen nothing like a study. He guessed "Uncle's study" was the summerhouse in the rear of the garden.

"Ynez . . . ?" he called up.

"Yes?"

"I love English gardens. Do you mind if I roam around?"

"Not at all. Make yourself at home."

He didn't head directly to the summerhouse, but meandered through the manicured hedges and tall, stately trees first.

Once he looked up at the cottage's second floor. He caught Ynez's eye in the window and she waved. He smiled, waved back, and moved on.

AXE and London Central had given him a complete line on Professor Harvey Raymond. Early on, the man had been a hard-liner against the State of Israel. He had also done several exhaustive studies on the Palestinian refugee problem. Even as late as a year earlier, he had written an article that partially condoned the extremes of terrorism in the world as a propaganda tool for Third-World countries.

Taken individually, the facets and facts of Harvey Raymond's life and views were not very different than a great many other British intellectuals. But lumped into a whole and puzzled out as a pattern, they stamped the man as more than a nodding friend of one or all the Arab movements dedicated to eradicating the Jewish state.

The summerhouse was sealed up like a tomb. There

were drop-lock hinges on each window, and a double dead-bolt on the single door. Carter could have gotten in, but it would have taken a little time, and the upstairs window of the cottage had a clear view of the summerhouse door.

He took a gravel path beyond the house and then, out of sight of the window, doubled back. In the rear he had to stretch to his toes to look in through the double, curtained windows.

The summerhouse was one large room, with a bathroom off a small alcove. The interior was dark; the walls, where there were no bookcases, dark wood. A mammoth oriental rug seemed to float on a sea of dark parquet. In the center was a large eighteenth-century desk. Beside it sat a smaller table with an electric typewriter on it. Books, raw manuscripts, and random papers were stashed everywhere on the floor and the desk.

Carter sighed with exasperation. There was very little he could learn on the outside looking in, and there was no time to get in.

He started back around the corner, and suddenly stopped. The house was half-timbered stucco, with full timbers running up all four corners. On this corner was a television antenna. Its stem started about four feet from the ground and ran up to about three feet above the roof line.

Something was wrong, didn't jive. The wings of the aerial weren't high enough above the roof, let alone the tree line. Also, the tube holding the couplers was as big as his wrist, when it only needed to be the diameter of his thumb at the most.

He trotted back to the window.

Bookshelves for indentations, possible cabinets, even the desk itself, and the ceiling area. Nowhere in the room did he see anything resembling a television set, or a piece of furniture or wall space that would hide one.

His mind clicked back to an Oxford professor he had heard comment years before on the mass medium of the tube: "Telly? . . . Good God, it's only for those who have less than enough brainpower to use the time on their hands, or prisoners in solitary confinement with no access to a library!"

Quickly, yanking a Swiss army knife from his pocket, Carter returned to the aerial. In seconds he had the base screws undone and was gently pulling the outer tube and its inner guts out from the timber.

One quick look told him. The six, finger-thick cables inside the casing had nothing to do with a television antenna. Not only that, but the coupling connections on each of them were designated in Cyrillic.

The Killmaster wasn't positive, but he was willing to lay long odds that the cables he was looking at didn't lead to a television but to a high-powered squirt transmitter.

He memorized the Russian identification numbers, and quickly screwed the whole of the tubing back into the timber.

By the time he returned to the cottage, Ynez was waiting for him in the kitchen, dressed, a small bag on the table.

"My, my," Carter said, grasping her by the shoulders, "dress you up and I could take you anywhere."

She pouted. "Is that an insult?"

"Quite the contrary. You look lovely."

And she did, in a mink coat over a two-piece knit dress that clung to her firm young body. Hatless, her dark hair was pulled back and very shiny. She had added just enough makeup so that she still looked engagingly fresh while adding a touch of mature mystery to her natural beauty.

"What I mean is, you look very different from the gypsy café hippie I met in Spain."

"Is that good or bad?"

He slid his arm around her waist and grabbed the bag. "A little of both . . . I hope."

She smiled up at him. "Thank you for coming, Nick. I'm glad you did, and I'm looking forward to a glorious evening."

"It will be," he said, not looking directly at her. "And we may even surprise Gerald before it's over."

It took only fifteen minutes for Harvey Raymond to make his decision after finding the note Ynez had left. It might be pure coincidence that the American agent, Nick Carter, had shown up in the English countryside and "dropped by" to see his niece, but the old professor didn't like the feel of it.

Certain phrases in the note had set off warning bells in his head: "staying the night with Gerald" . . . "sorry he missed you, would like to meet you" . . . "knows Gerald, met him at a party or two . . ."

With the operation in Luxembourg moving so fast, nothing could now be overlooked.

When the computer was warmed up, Raymond typed in the message directly from his head. After explaining everything in detail, he went back and underlined the last phrase for emphasis.

Imperative, repeat, imperative: if action is taken, all procedures to insure safety of female must be taken. Repeat, this must be stressed.

This done, he set the frequency and activated the key-through that would feed the full message from the computer to the transmitter.

It took only seconds for the electronic transformer to warm to maximum. When it did, he depressed the red button.

The message was three hundred or so words, about sixteen hundred characters. It took to the air in a scrambled squirt that took 1/1000 of a second to transmit.

The needle had scarcely settled back to zero when the old man shut down the transmitter, rotated the aerial with a hand crank from inside the house, and activated the receiver.

A half cup of tea later, the reply came and was automatically unscrambled on the computer screen.

Transmission received. Will treat with utmost priority London. Understand caution and will comply.

The restaurant was tiny and in one of the more disreputable areas of Southwark near the Thames. By American standards it was little more than a greasy spoon with a printed menu, but Carter loved it and they served the best fillet of sole in London.

The dessert and coffee had come and gone. Now they were lingering over brandy.

By mutual agreement, they had passed on seeing a show. A leisurely dinner and talk suited both their moods.

Shortly after arriving, Carter had excused himself and called London AXE. The duty officer had assured him that he would have the information on the Russian numbers back in less than an hour.

Ynez called Gerald Raymond's flat to inform her cousin that she was in town and would be staying the night. While she was gone, Carter found himself hoping that Raymond would indeed be in the flat and sick in bed. It wouldn't simplify matters, but it would put some of his suspicions to rest.

"No answer," she said when she returned to the table.

"Oh?"

"He was probably called out somewhere on business. He brokers for importers, you know."

"No," Carter said, "I didn't know."

"No matter. I have a key to the flat." Here she laughed. "It was my flat in the first place. It's still in my name."

That, Carter thought, was why he could find no known address on Gerald Raymond.

Another piece in place.

He sat across the table from her, looking at her in the glow of the table lamp. Her face was finely shaped, delicately boned, but inexpressive and immobile at the moment, as if she were deep in her own thoughts.

Carter didn't know what she was thinking, but he knew what he was thinking and he had a twinge of conscience about it.

He had already started the ball rolling, playing on her loneliness. Three aperitifs before dinner, a bottle of wine during, and now a brandy. It was already showing in her speech and in her heavy-lidded, long-lashed eyes.

A burly waiter in a black apron to avoid showing the dirt appeared beside the table. "Your name Carter?"

"Yes."

"Telephone, pay box by the door."

"Excuse me."

It was London AXE.

"Carter here."

"Checked out your numbers and they refer to both a transmitter and a receiver. It's a high-powered Soviet LMF-270, very handy little piece of gear."

"Did you check with MI5?"

"I did. Portsmouth and Glasgow have picked up squirt transmissions from that area of the Cotswolds before, but they haven't been able to get a fix. The transmissions are infrequent and they don't have any particular time. Also, one of their experts told me the sender could have an alternate booster antenna hidden somewhere miles away that bounces the signal."

"Just how powerful is this LMF-270?" Carter asked.

"On a clear night, under the right atmospheric conditions, he could be heard loud and clear in Moscow."

"Thanks, I'll be back to you."

The Killmaster hung up and headed back to the table. Now it was more important than ever that he spend a little time in Gerald Raymond's apartment.

If Harvey Raymond's transmissions could be heard in Moscow, then they could surely be copied in Tripoli, Libya.   ·

"It's getting late. I'll take you home."

Ynez shrugged and walked with him to the door.

"You look grim . . . bad news?"

"Maybe. I won't know for a while yet."

He paid the check and rejoined her at the door. They were just leaving when the cashier opened the door behind them and called, "Mr. Carter, another call!"

"I'll meet you at the car." He moved back inside and picked up the receiver. "Yeah?"

"MI5 just called. They want to know why you asked."

"Any special reason?" Carter replied.

"Yeah, your man just squirted again."

"When?" Carter asked, little men starting to pound in his head.

"About forty minutes ago. What should I tell 'em?"

"That I'll get up with them."

The car was parked near the Embankment. He nearly missed it in the fog. Ynez wasn't standing beside it, so he lit a cigarette and moved to the wall.

"Got another one?"

She moved out of the fog and stood close, her arm moving through his. He looked down at her and smiled.

"I think we've played this scene before, in Spain?"

She returned the smile. "Same scene, different fog. Where are you staying tonight?"

She was close enough so he could see the damp brilliance of her eyes and inhale the sharp sweetness of her scent.

"My company maintains a flat in Mayfair."

She laughed. "Your company?" She jostled Wilhelmina with the back of her hand. "Why don't you lie to me and tell me your 'company' makes refrigerators or tellys?"

"No, I won't do that."

"Good."

She stood on tiptoe and slid her arms around his neck. He put his arms around her and she clung to him, raising her face sweetly, almost like a child . . . but a child with a woman's body. Carter leaned down and kissed her, and the response was sudden, explosive.

"Do you have to stay in your company apartment tonight?"

"No."

That was it. They walked hand in hand to the car.

Easy, Carter thought, handing her in and walking around to the driver's side. *I only hope it's spur of the moment and not designed.*

THIRTEEN

The apartment was on the Strand, in an older building on the river side. It had two-bedrooms with a high-ceilinged living room in the center. It was small but chic. There were a few very good pieces of old country furniture against white walls, bare except for a couple of striking abstracts, a corner fireplace, a chaste, modern couch, and a large window that would have framed a superlative view of the city had it been a clear night.

"Nice," Carter said, forcing himself not to look like a dime-store detective or a fire inspector.

"Would you like a drink?"

"No."

"Would you like me?"

"Yes."

She smiled for real now. "My bedroom is on this side."

The next few minutes became a haze as he followed her into the bedroom and they both stood silently, each undressing the other.

"You have a difficult line of work," she said, delicate fingers tracing the scars on his body.

"I fell out of a tree as a child."

Then they were on the bed, the dark tan of his body blending with her naturally olive-toned skin. He twisted her head so her mouth came up to meet his. It was a savage kiss. Her breasts were crushed against his chest and both arms clung desperately about his neck and a low moan escaped from her throat. Her head fell back away from him limply and her eyes were closed, her face peaceful now with a strange look of content.

"Hurry," she whispered. "I don't want to change my mind."

"You mean you might?"

"No . . . yes, no . . . oh, hell, I don't know."

A shudder traversed the length of her body. She opened her eyes to his gaze and there was a little girl pleading in them.

Carter turned to lower her unresisting body back onto the bed. She lay back limply and closed her eyes again. A tremulous smile fluttered across her lips. He lay beside her and lowered his face within inches of hers. She lay with eyes closed, quiescent and waiting, only the gradual increase in the tempo of her breathing betraying the inner excitement gripping her.

Carter kissed each eyelid gently. He moved his mouth down her cheek to the slightly parted lips and across them. She began to shudder again and her hands reached for him.

They came together fiercely, locking at once in a tight union. Ynez writhed, gasping and whimpering alternately.

Carter didn't know if the whimpers were caused only by desire, or also, to some extent, by pain, since the joining of their bodies had been sudden and forceful.

He needn't have been concerned, however. It soon became obvious that the woman was experiencing excruciating pleasure. She began to grind her hips and toss and roll back and forth against him. The extreme friction was thrilling.

He went at her avidly, not permitting her size to slow him. He hurt her, he knew. But he also knew that she liked it. Her clawing hands told him that, as did her wild little cries and the drumming of her heels. He bucked up and down and felt himself ascending the mountain far faster than was usual for him. He stopped moving.

"Don't!" she shrieked. *"Keep going!"* A sob exploded from her.

He started up again. She tossed herself against and around him all the stronger, and he knew that there was no stopping then. He only hoped that Ynez would be with him when they tumbled over the passion crest.

As he upped the tempo, she emitted a sharp "Ah! Ah!" Then she cried out loudly and seemed to rise to him in an ascending spiral.

He finished at the next instant, and it was sharply explosive. When he came to rest on his elbows, to protect her slim body from his full weight, her arms and legs were limp as those of a rag doll.

Slipping from the bedroom, Carter closed the door soundlessly behind him. Even though he knew the girl, in her present state, would sleep through anything short of a tornado, he made as little noise as possible searching.

The living room offered nothing. Even the few books and personal items could have belonged to anyone.

Gerald Raymond's bedroom also smacked of someone very transient. The furniture was Spartan and the desk top was clean. A locked drawer yielded nothing but a pile of ledgers listing purchases, sales, and commissions on everything from Moroccan rugs to brass teapots.

Evidently Raymond did in fact dabble in the import-export trade.

Several hand-tailored suits, a rack of ties, and three pieces of expensive luggage were all he found in the closet.

Carter knew the luggage, and knew that that set had three bags. Unless Raymond traveled with a very small bag, he hadn't packed anything on his current trip.

The dresser's contents was equally sparse: a few shirts, socks, and some underwear. The contents of his jewelry box was expensive but not lavish.

Another ten minutes of looking at what could have been hiding places revealed nothing more than a rack of shoes beneath the bed.

Carter stood in the center of the room, slowly turning full around.

Gerald Raymond had expensive tastes but lived in a Spartan atmosphere. It was as if the shirts, suits, and shoes were used rather than worn. It was the trappings of a man using a cover, as if the clothes were a skin to be shed or put on when necessary.

It was obvious that Raymond occupied this room, but did he *live* here?

Did he live anywhere? Or was he just passing through life, and a small part of it was spent here?

The only personal items in the room was a row of framed photos on the small mantel. One by one, Carter picked them up and examined them.

There was a shot of Raymond and Ynez, posing formally in front of the Cotswold cottage. They were both in their teens. Another was Raymond with a tall, gaunt, gray-haired man. Both were smiling, and Raymond was dressed in a dark graduation gown. Carter guessed the older man was Uncle Harvey.

There was a ravishing shot of Ynez posed in an off-the-shoulder gown, inscribed "I will always look up to you and adore you, dear Gerald . . . Ynez."

Carter was about to set the photograph down, when he noticed two edges along the bottom where it was slipped into the frame. Using his fingernails, he tugged until a second picture, under the photo of Ynez, slipped out.

It was of three people, a broad-shouldered, slightly graying man, a handsome, dark-eyed woman, and a young boy with clear bright eyes and a mop of black hair that curled down over his forehead.

Carter stared and stared at the picture. Something about it was jogging his memory. The old car? The whitewashed house with the stark hills in the background?

He crossed the room and snapped on the bedside lamp.

The woman was beautiful, but Carter was sure he had never seen her before. And the man could have been . . . any Arab.

Suddenly he froze, flipping the photograph over. On the back was a photographer's signature, stamped, and above it, in ink in Arabic script with a precise, feminine hand, was written, "Leila and Omar Rahman, Ja'il, aged 8."

Carter flipped it back over and brought it up close to his eyes. For a full minute he squinted at the boy, and then let his eyes close.

It came back. The traitor in Summa, Abu Rahman. The young boy, his back torn to shreds by splinters. The mountain at the first light of dawn, binding the boy's wounds with the torn djellaba.

No matter. I will have to kill my uncle.

The frail, almost naked body standing at the mouth of the cave.

You have saved my life, Nick Carter, American. I thank you.

Now the Killmaster knew why he had not been blown to hell along with the Audi.

He replaced the picture in the frame and reset it on the mantel. Then he slipped back into the other bedroom. In the moonlight from the window he found Ynez's purse. From it he withdrew her wallet.

In the fourth plastic window he flipped, he found a smiling head shot of Ja'il Rahman as he was today: Gerald Raymond.

Ynez slept on soundlessly as he dressed and scribbled her a quick note.

He waited until he was in the hall before slipping on his shoes. Then he hurried down the street and jogged toward the rental car.

As he ran, he went over in his mind what he would do with the picture, and how much good he hoped would come out of it.

The street was quiet, deserted. His mind was distracted. That was why the thud on the roof of the car and the following whine froze him for an instant, instead of galvanizing him into action.

The second slug jerked at his coat, and Carter felt a burning sensation across his left arm and wrist.

That moved him. He lurched across the street and then went into a dive toward the opposite walk. He hit the cement with a breath-pounding jolt, digging under his coat for Wilhelmina.

At the same time, a third slug whined off the cement a foot from his head.

But this time he saw the rifle, the orange spray flared even more than normal because of the silencer. It came from an office building across the street, third floor, corner window.

Carter was up and running in the shadows. Another slug

hit the pavement but several feet away.

He hit the door and found it locked. He tried kicking it, but it was too solid. It did have a small glass pane. Using the solid butt of the Luger, he broke it out, reached in, and unlocked the door.

Inside was a small alcove and a stairway leading up. He took it three steps at a time.

Third floor. The window with the flashes had been on the third floor, corner.

He stopped at the second-floor landing and listened. It was an entire floor devoted to small offices—lawyers, a dentist, a copy service, a secretarial pool—all closed down and dark.

He heard nothing but the sound of his own breathing and his working heart pounding blood through his system at a few hundred miles per.

He left the hallway that led down to the second-floor offices and moved up the stairs, the Luger ahead of him, a live round in the chamber and the safety off, his finger on the trigger with a slight pressure. There would be no time. When—if—it came, there would be no time for anything but just one quick reaction.

He reached the third-floor landing. It was a duplicate of the second. Small offices on either side of a long hallway, at the end a fire exit.

Carter paused, studying it. Everything was still, almost peaceful. Had the guy already made it out of the building? He could have gone down the fire escape.

Sound, the slight scrape of a chair, from one of the offices near the end of the hallway to his right.

He moved forward in a crouch, keeping to the left, the Luger ready and out to the right, waist high.

Just as he reached the door, there was a sudden movement behind him and carpet sound. He wheeled, his finger taking up the slack on the trigger.

He'd been suckered. Yeah, the first shooter was in the office, but he had two backups waiting in one of the offices Carter had just passed.

If the shooter didn't get him on the street, they wanted him to come up after him. Ten to one there was another one of them down on the street in a car somewhere.

The two behind him were rolling out of an open door when Carter fired. He caught the upright one with two in his middle. His gun clattered to the floor and he toppled forward, trying to hold his guts in.

Number two was more dangerous. He had a shotgun and was all set to spray. He was also lying flat out, which made it a much harder shot.

So instead of shooting, Carter did just the opposite. He let go with an ear-piercing wail and ran forward directly at the man.

Just as the barrel of the shotgun came up, Carter launched. He went flying over the prone body as the shotgun roared. The pellets smashed glass and plaster all down the hall, and Carter came down on his side. He rolled and came to one knee, firing.

He emptied the magazine all along the length of the man's body, not caring what he hit just so long as he did hit.

He did.

Two screams and silence.

Carter holstered Wilhelmina and grabbed the shotgun. As he ran he pumped a hot shell into the chamber.

He came down the hallway opposite the door where he had heard the shifting chair. When he reached it, he raised his foot, kicked it in, and fell forward on his stomach. From carpet level he swept the room.

Nothing.

He was in an entry cubicle that led into a lot of chrome and leather. Carter was about to rise, when he heard the fire exit door slam open.

He was up and running, holding the shotgun at port. The fire door was open. Carter went through and fell into a crouch. His man was between the first floor and the street, taking the steps five at a time.

Impossible shot.

He started down himself. By the time he was at the first-floor landing, his man was loping up the alley toward the street. Carter stopped, balanced the shotgun on the fire escape's iron railing, and fired.

There was a scream and the man flew forward, doing a perfect four-point into some garbage cans.

Carter took off again. In the distance he could hear sirens. In the alley he saw his quarry pulling himself to his feet and stumbling forward.

The distance had been too great for the shotgun to make a complete kill. But in the light of a streetlight Carter could see that it had been a hit. Most of the man's jacket and shirt had been blown away and his back looked like raw hamburger.

Carter wiped the shotgun free of his prints as he ran and tossed it away. There had already been too much noise.

By the time he hit the street, the wounded man was heading toward a black sedan half a block away, its engine already revved up and whining.

The car's light came on as Carter steadied the Luger on the running figure. Its beams flashed into his eyes, making him squint.

Just as he was about to fire, the front of the car lifted and the rear tires screeched. The screaming of the tires was nothing compared to the scream of the wounded man as he was smashed forward and thrown to the pavement. By the time the sedan's rear wheels had passed over his body, he was silent.

So much for honor among brothers in terror, Carter thought, as the sedan shot on down the street.

And so much, he thought, as he ran like hell for his own car, *for Ja'il keeping me alive!*

FOURTEEN

Carter stood at one of the castle's upper, slitted windows, looking out at the bright sun glinting off the previous night's snowfall.

It was nearly noon and he had spent the whole morning, after only two hours' sleep, going over the rest of security. The little things they hadn't covered on the night of his abortive raid, they had gone over in minute detail that morning.

After the mess in London, he had phoned AXE Central and told them the cleanup would best be handled by British MI5. Also, he wanted a rundown on identities and background of the bodies.

The AXE duty officer had almost blown his stack. "Christ, Carter, if you don't let these people in on just what war you're fighting, they're not going to give you crap."

"I'm about to do that," Carter had answered calmly. "I've got two hours before I get a plane back to Brussels. In that time, I'm bringing a photograph in. I want it duplicated and passed all over the U.K. and Europe, especially the Luxembourg frontiers. I'll take a good-sized stack of them back with me for Schloss Valkyrie security."

The man calmed down. "You think you've got your man?"

"I haven't got him, but I've got a damned good line on him. The subject in the Cotswolds is one Harvey Raymond. He's a guest lecturer at Cambridge and an expert on the Middle East. My guess is MI5 has a dossier on him. If they haven't, pass on the one that we've put together in the last few days."

"Got it."

"Now, this is important. I want surveillance only on this Harvey Raymond. No bugs, no arrests, and hopefully no leak that we're on to him. That's top-priority important. If they kick, tell them to contact me at the Schloss Valkyrie and I'll put a NATO fire under their ass. Okay?"

"Right on. Anything else?"

"Yeah. Get the records of every airline flying in and out of Algiers for the past year. I want to know if a British citizen was on any of those flights, name of Gerald Raymond."

There was a moan from the other end of the line. *"Every* flight?"

"Every seat on every flight."

"Good God."

Carter chuckled. "That's what computers are for, pal."

Now every frontier guard and every security person at the castle had a photograph of Gerald Raymond. Carter didn't have much hope that it would do any good, but at least they were trying.

Peter Reinbold's voice, seated at a table behind Carter in the center of the room, brought him out of his reverie. "Then you're satisfied with what I've done so far?"

"Hell, yes," Carter said. "You've done a fine job, Peter. I just have a gut feeling it's all a waste of time."

"Come on, Nick, how so? My God, this place is tighter than your Fort Knox."

"So was Troy . . . they thought."

Carter got himself a cup of coffee, lit a cigarette, and joined Reinbold at the table.

"Look, we've got the perimeter controlled. The air space above this castle is out. There will be two choppers in the air twenty-four hours a day."

Carter nodded. "So far, so good."

"The night before the meeting, the conference room will be swept. The dogs will be brought in to sniff for explosives, and then the room will be sealed and nobody gets in until the meeting itself. What more can we do?"

Carter shrugged and sipped his coffee. "Pray."

Reinbold groaned and threw up his hands. "You still think he'll try?"

"You're damned right I do. If I didn't before, I do now. That try for me in London was for real. They know I'm here and I'm poking. If this Ja'il doesn't come at us from the outside, he'll do it from the inside."

"Nick, I'm telling you it's impossible!" Reinbold blurted in frustration. He waited for Carter to reply, and when he didn't, continued. "All right, if you're so sure, tell me what more I can do."

"I've already told you and everybody else who will listen. Convince the Israelis and the Arabs to invite Hassan Al-Chir. He won't blow himself to hell."

Reinbold dropped his head into his hands. "We're still trying."

"Any results?"

"My government and yours have agreed. So have the French."

"But not the Arabs and the Israelis."

Reinbold's lips curved in a humorless smile. "Have you

ever known them to agree on anything? But we're still trying."

"Mark my words," Carter growled, rising again and walking to the window, "you'd better try harder."

The telephone rang and Reinbold grabbed it. The conversation was short and terse. When he hung up, he spoke to Carter.

"That was Bonn. They haven't got a lead on Bretoff, but they've located his girlfriend in Wiesbaden. She's hoisting steins in a beer hall. Why so interested in Bretoff?"

"Because this Ja'il is a bomb man. He likes specialty stuff like Gelemax. Gunter Bretoff has been the major source of Gelemax in Germany and most of Europe since the Baader-Meinhoff days."

"Maybe so, Nick, but no one has heard a whisper from Bretoff since he went underground two years ago."

"That doesn't mean he isn't still in business. If Ja'il is going to use Gelemax, he'll try to buy it at the source, in Germany. It's too difficult and dangerous to transport long distances, and he's cautious. That's how he's stayed clean all these years. Peter . . . ?"

"*Ja?*"

"What's with all the vans down there?"

The German joined him at the window and stared down at the vast courtyard teeming with vans and people.

"Three of them are ours, unmarked and painted a neutral color. That one is the caterer's. We decided to bring the food in. That way we don't have to use a kitchen staff. Our own security people will act as waiters. Don't worry about them. Frau Baunstaffer has them all checked out, down to the salad chef and the dishwasher."

"Who belongs to the blue one?"

"Furniture people. They're taking a table to be refinished and some legs repaired." Here Reinbold laughed.

"What's so funny?" Carter asked.

"Zigmann, the custodian. I had to get between him and Frau Baunstaffer this morning. The old man claims he did a fine job on the table and sending it out is a waste of time and money."

Carter smiled. "Evidently the woman won."

"She usually does. I think that's another reason old Zigmann battles with her. Besides hating women in general, he can't stand having one for a boss."

Carter wandered back to the table and gazed down at the mass of paper detailing every facet of the elaborate security setup.

"Okay, Peter," he sighed, "let's go through it all again. There's always a hole, somewhere."

Peter Reinbold groaned and popped into his mouth his tenth antacid tablet of the morning.

The small café was on Route 49, about a mile from the Luxembourg frontier toward Trier in Germany. It was crowded with Swiss, Germans, and a sprinkling of Frenchmen.

Gerald Raymond, in the workingman's clothes that had become like a second skin to him, stood at the bar sipping coffee.

Through the front window, he saw the white van pull up and the driver get out.

Hans Raab was a short, wide man with a face the color of raw beef who walked solidly on the thick soles of square-toed black boots. His very broad shoulders were bulkily emphasized in the tight blue coveralls he wore. A matching blue, billed cap was shoved back on his balding head from a sweating brow. Even though it was freezing outside, he wore no jacket.

Raymond's stomach took a little jump as Raab came through the door. He had only worked with the man peripherally, but he knew a great deal about him.

Raab was efficient, tops at whatever he did, loyal to the point of puppy-doggishness, and a thorough sadist.

Raymond guessed that the worst part of this job for Raab would be not being able to see the mangled bodies the bomb they were about to plant would create.

He paused a few steps into the room and looked around, from face to face. When his eyes found Raymond, they paused. Raymond broke a thin cigar in half. He put one half in his pocket and lit the other, then took his coffee to a nearby table.

Raab sat at a vacant table next to his and ordered coffee. For several minutes they sat, sipping, not even looking at one another.

"Excuse me," the big man said, getting up and reaching across Raymond's table for an extra sugar cube. In the process he dropped a key in Raymond's coffee.

One swallow and, with the key in his mouth, Raymond rose. He paid his bill and walked outside. The van was parked with the rear end of it away from the café.

Within five seconds of disappearing behind it, Raymond had used the key and was inside. By the time Raab crawled into the driver's seat and started the engine, Raymond was also in a pair of blue coveralls.

"I expected a much younger man."

Raymond only grunted. Good, he thought, the disguise was working. He might not have to kill the big German after all.

"You have the explosives?"

Again Raymond didn't reply. He pulled up the legs of both his coveralls and his own trousers to reveal the packets of Gelemax taped to his legs.

Raab leered. "I like Gelemax."

Raymond looked up for the first time into Hans Raab's clear blue eyes. He saw mirrored there such depths of sheer depravity that he felt revulsion. Those eyes were old with sin and with hatred for his fellow man.

Raymond decided he would kill Raab after all, if for no other reason than to cleanse whatever conscience he had left.

"Which toolboxes?" Raymond grunted.

"The two black ones. The false bottoms are released by turning the lid release three extra times to the right. Find it?"

"Yes."

"The grease and garlic solution is in the white kit by your foot."

Raymond spread it carefully over each packet of Gelemax, and then placed that packet in the false bottom of one of the toolboxes. By the time they had reached the frontier, the job was done and Raymond was in the passenger seat puffing on his cigar.

Serge Gussman was German. He had done various odd jobs for Hassan Al-Chir over the past two years. This was the strangest job he had ever done, but in many ways the easiest and most profitable. The two Turks he had hired to help him he had gotten for pennies. Raab worked directly for Al-Chir, so Gussman wouldn't have to cut him in at all.

It was a snap.

Gussman listened to the woman on the other end of the line.

"The woman has followed instructions. The table has been delivered. You'll get a call sometime late tomorrow evening if the release is go. Do you understand?"

"I do."

The phone went dead.

Gussman lowered the telephone gently to its cradle. He stood without moving for a moment, thick shoulders hunched forward slightly, straining the seams of his carefully tailored tweed jacket. He had smooth, chubby features with a deep cleft in his chin that gave him a deceptive look of almost innocent boyishness. Until you looked into his eyes. They were neither innocent nor boyish.

Gussman's eyes were round and slightly protuberant. They were such a light blue as to appear almost white, an effect that was heightened by fragmentary brows so blond that they were practically invisible. The result was curious and somehow frightening.

Gussman pulled a ski mask over his face and walked into the bedroom. It was an ordinary bedroom with the sort of furniture that comes with a rented house. The gray light of late afternoon came through a single window to illuminate the bed on which the girl lay.

She lay on her side with her face toward Gussman, twisting and straining futilely against the belt buckled around her knees and the length of clothesline that bound her wrists behind her back. A bathroom sponge was jammed into her mouth for a gag, held in place by a soiled handkerchief bound around her head.

Disheveled dark hair was splayed about her face, and one eye blazed with anger at him and the other two men in the room, who leaned casually against the opposite wall, idly chewing on matchsticks and watching her struggles with the impersonal interest of two scientists observing an impaled specimen.

Her face was pale and drawn. Even with the anger in her eyes, she looked like a child. But the breast that had escaped from the ripped print dress and lay exposed was as round and full as that of a mature woman.

One of the Turks leaning against the wall moved his head a fraction of an inch in her direction and spoke past the matchstick between his teeth. "Some nice stuff there."

Gussman spoke dispassionately. "She's only seventeen years old, you pig." Gussman hated Turks. He would rather kill these two than pay them off, but it would pose too large a problem getting rid of the bodies.

"Hell of a body for seventeen."

Gussman ignored him and stepped to the bed to look down at the girl speculatively. "Can you breathe all right?"

She nodded.

"Are you hungry?"

She shook her head.

"Your mother did as she was told. You should be free in a couple of days." He turned to the two Turks. "Follow me."

They did, closing the door behind them. Gussman stopped at the table and began counting out two stacks of money.

"You are sure you don't want us to stay around and help you dump her off?"

"I'm sure," Gussman replied, handing them the money. "Your part is done. Both of you get back to Frankfurt and stay there."

They shrugged and headed for the door. Gussman peeled off his ski mask and spoke again just as they stepped outside.

"And, both of you, listen good," he said, his voice guttural. "Forget this. Even if you get picked up for something, don't remember this."

As one, both men shrank away from the distilled vitriol that dripped from his thick lips.

They didn't have to ask what would happen if they remembered. As one, they ran for their car.

The sound of the engine had barely died away when Gussman set about arranging Therese Baunstaffer's "escape."

FIFTEEN

Early-afternoon cloud cover had drifted in by the time Hans Raab and Gerald Raymond reached the guarded perimeter of the Schloss Valkyrie and had their credentials gone over scrupulously by three stern BfV men.

"Drive on into the courtyard," the last one said, waving them through the tall iron gates. "But go no further until you have seen Frau Baunstaffer."

Raab drove slowly up the cobbled lane and into the huge courtyard. As Raab conferred with the inner gate sentry, Raymond looked to the sky and allowed a tiny smile to crease his newly aged lips.

The cloud cover reached farther than the eye could see now, completely blocking out what little heat the sun had beamed down earlier. It would be bitterly cold up on the roof.

Raab called out to him in the stern voice a journeyman would use to his assistant. "Get the tools and materials out of the truck. They have to be gone over by the dogs."

Raymond nodded and opened the rear door of the van. By the time he had the materials and the toolboxes spread

out on the ground, another officer was bringing up two
German shepherds. For a full ten minutes the two men, the
materials, and the open toolboxes were sniffed and re-
sniffed.

"Nothing," the man replied, leading the dogs away.

Raymond let the little knot that had formed in the center
of his gut unfurl. The very worst hurdle was over. The
combined grease and garlic oil had shielded the distinctive
scent of the Gelemax from the dogs.

Raab was calling him over. A tall woman with a thin
figure, slightly graying hair, and harried features was going
over their papers.

"The dogs found nothing?"

"No, Frau Baunstaffer."

The woman turned an appraising eye their way. "You
are not the same two who were here before, the ones who
botched the job?"

"*Nein,*" Raab replied. "That is why we are here."

"Let's do it right this time," she barked, handing their
papers back, turning to the sentries. "One of you help them
carry their supplies up to the roof, and, as usual, stay with
them."

The two men exchanged a quick, guarded look as they
hoisted their toolboxes. They had both noticed the little
twitch at the corner of the woman's eye and the slight
shake in her hands. They also knew that their security
check and interrogation had been more formality than substance.

Frau Ilse Baunstaffer was far more worried about the
table she had sent out that morning than she was about the
patching of a roof.

As Raymond walked up the stone stairs toward the roof,
he glanced to his left. There, behind a large bay window,
staring directly at him, was Nick Carter.

He tensed for only a fraction of a second, and then relaxed as he remembered Leba Fani's near genius at makeup.

He also noticed that Carter was not looking at him. The man was preoccupied, looking straight through him.

"It's for you," Reinbold said, extending the telephone, "as usual."

Carter crossed to the desk and grabbed the instrument. "This is Carter."

"Nick, Jarvis Whitney, London."

Carter sighed and then chuckled. Whitney was the head of AXE Central, London. He was glad they had brought in the first team.

"Yeah, Jarvis, what have you got?"

"Looks like you're on the right track with this Raymond character. He flew into Algiers three times last year ... February, July, and November. Also twice this year, and the last time was eight days ago."

"Go on," Carter said, the dark, curly hair and the chiseled features swimming in front of his eyes.

"He has an import-export license for the U.K., and he did make buys while he was there, but nothing that would support the expense of the trip. Also, MI5 did a check on his bank accounts—expenditures, taxes, the works."

"And," Carter growled, "he doesn't make enough to support his life-style."

"Exactly. Financially, he's about on the same level as a shoe salesman. Impossible, on his income, to travel the way he does."

"What about the old man, Harvey Raymond?"

"Under surveillance. He hasn't moved. They managed a tap on the phone, but all he's called is his garage."

"Thanks for the info on Raymond, Jarvis. Stay with it."

"Will do."

Carter hung up and turned to Reinbold. "Gerald Raymond is our man."

The big German nodded. "Now all we have to do is find the bastard."

They had the tiles removed and set aside. Just as they had both hoped, the sentry who had come up with them had retreated to the cover of a nearby chimney to get out of the freezing wind.

Raab had the kerosene heater going strong, and the roofing tar was bubbling nicely above it. There had been one tough moment to get through, when the tiles were removed while the sentry was still standing over them. A blind man could see the large spot in the dried tar that had been eaten away by the acid.

The sentry had barely glanced at it and then burrowed his face deeper into the wraparound collar of his heavy coat.

"How close?" Raab asked.

"Just a few more minutes. I'm almost down to the layer next to the wood. Bring it out and start kneading it."

Raymond continued digging at the dried tar with a flat trowel while the German lifted each cake of Gelemax, one at a time, from the false bottom of the toolboxes.

Every now and then he glanced up at the sentry as he flattened each chunk of explosive out on a tile and then laid it aside like a pancake.

"Splash a little tar on each one for color as you finish," Raymond murmured.

"I am. Shit!"

Both men looked up. One of the wrappers had blown from Raab's hand and flown across the roof. As they watched, it swirled in the wind and then flattened itself against the stone not six inches from the sentry's shoulder.

"Fool," Raymond hissed, "stay here!"

He stood and teetered across the stationary tiles and over the peak to the chimney. As he moved he took a cigar from his pocket and peeled it.

"Could I get a light from you?"

"What?... Oh, sure."

The sentry produced a lighter and both men bent together as a shield over it. Carefully, Raymond sneaked a hand up over the other man's shoulder and walked his fingers along the stone until they touched the paper.

Gently he pulled it into his fist and wadded it.

"Thank you."

"How much longer? This wind keeps up, they'll find us frozen up here come spring."

Raymond laughed. "Another half hour at the most."

Back with Raab, he slipped him the wrapper. "Burn the paper in the heater as you unwrap the stuff."

Raab gritted his teeth and went back to work.

Fifteen minutes later they were ready with the pancakes of Gelemax. Carefully, they laid them out until there were none left.

"All right," Raymond said, "time to share a cup of coffee with our friend there."

Raab grabbed a thermos and headed across the roof. Raymond went to work.

From a large flashlight, he extracted two small batteries and carefully bound them together with black electrical tape. Gingerly, he mashed a metal tube filled with fulminate down into the Gelemax. This was the detonator. An insulated lead wire, dead, was run from the detonator across the layer of Gelemax to an open space that would be covered by a series of tiles.

Then he took a common Accutron watch from his wrist.

The watch wasn't running because its tiny transistor battery had been removed.

He attached the detonator wire to the hand mechanism of the wristwatch. Then, using finer wire, he very carefully attached the receiver to the battery terminals of the watch.

The last thing was to attach the batteries to the receiver and test it.

No problem.

When the time came, Raymond would activate the receiver from a place in the village they had already chosen. The receiver, run by the batteries, would set the minute hand in motion. Thirty minutes later it would hit the hour mark, letting the charge from the batteries flow to the detonator. The fulminate would burn through and . . . boom.

"Are you going to drink coffee all day? I'm ready to replace the tiles!"

Raab quickly returned, and together they reset all the tiles in place.

"Will the weight of the tiles be enough?"

"More than enough," Raymond replied. "They will force the blast downward. Also, those two skylights will take care of anyone the blast misses. The whole room will be filled with flying glass."

Raab almost giggled.

Just before settling the last tile in place over the components, Raymond attached the aerial to the receiver.

"Could you give us a hand with the toolboxes?"

The sentry was only too happy to oblige. His lips and nose were turning blue.

As Raab and the sentry hauled the boxes across the roof, Raymond strung out the aerial. Carefully, he laid it along the tiles so it was impossible to see with the naked eye unless the observer was on his hands and knees less than a foot above it.

When the aerial was secured to the chimney, he rejoined Raab and the sentry on the climb down.

"I hope it's fixed now," the sentry said.

"Oh, it's fixed," Raab replied. "I doubt if it will give you any trouble for years."

Facts, figures, theories, suppositions, and a hundred other things running through Carter's mind awakened him.

His watch said midnight. He looked down, saw that he was fully clothed, and remembered.

Reinbold, Ilse Baunstaffer, and he had eaten an early dinner in the small alcove off the kitchen. All three of them had tried to be jovial and talked of everything except the approaching meeting and the security for it.

But, eventually, talk dwindled and the three of them had sat, silently sipping brandy, absorbed in their own thoughts.

Then the woman had started jabbering, almost aimlessly but with a common thread.

She had done everything she could do. She had faithfully carried out every duty assigned to her. She had come to the end of her rope, how could they expect more of her?

And then she had broken down in tears.

Reinbold had tried to comfort her. Carter had sat back and surveyed the situation with a jaundiced eye. He had gone over the files on everyone involved with anything at the castle. If anyone could be considered a rock of stability, including Peter Reinbold, it was Frau Ilse Baunstaffer.

Now, suddenly, she had done two things that didn't fit her background or her character profile. She had taken far too much to drink before, during, and after dinner, and she had broken down in tears.

Reinbold had insisted that she stay at the castle that night rather than return to her cottage in the village. Then he had escorted her to the room allotted her in the castle.

When he returned, Carter voiced his questions concerning the woman's stability.

"It's nothing. The woman has just been driving herself too hard. I've worked with her before . . . believe me, she is reliable."

The Killmaster accepted the explanation, but he wasn't convinced. Years of looking inside people told him that Ilse Baunstaffer was beginning to crack. And if she were cracking, he guessed that there was a bigger reason for it than overwork.

He opened his eyes wide and reached out a long arm for his lighter and a cigarette. Lighting it, he puffed heavily and watched the gray-blue whorls of smoke drift upward and float across the ceiling.

He forced thoughts of the woman from his mind and concentrated on Gerald Raymond. It all fit now, and even though he didn't know all of the details, he could piece most of the intervening years together.

That evening he had received a report from Israeli intelligence on the Summa debacle of twenty years before. A second report from MI5 on Raymond had brought it up to date.

The two reports, plus a detailed account of Hassan Al-Chir's terrorist activities through the years, cemented it.

Ja'il/Gerald had been the hand that had carried out Al-Chir's demonic plans—and probably masterminded many of them. The legend that had been built up as Hassan Al-Chir was, in fact, Gerald Raymond.

It was an impressive legend, and the reason Carter was now having so many doubts was that he was sure, no matter how tight their security or how many precautions they took, Raymond would find a way.

Groaning, he mashed out his cigarette and rolled his feet

to the floor. He was nearly undressed when the telephone buzzed. The button for the in-house connection was lit.

"Yeah?"

"Nick, we just got a call from Washington and a confirm from Brussels."

Sweat broke out on his forehead and, to his surprise, he found that the hand holding the telephone was shaking.

"Talk to me, Peter—tell me we've got an early Christmas present."

"It looks that way. Israel and the United Arab delegates agreed this afternoon. Contact was made in Libya earlier this evening."

"And . . .?"

"Brussels got the word about twenty minutes ago. Hassan Al-Chir has agreed to attend the meeting."

Carter whooshed out the air he'd been holding in his lungs. "Peter, we just might make it."

"Let's put it this way . . . we've got a hell of a lot more points on our side now. Get a good night's sleep for a change."

"I do believe I will," Carter chuckled.

He slid under the thick down quilt with just that in mind for the first night in several.

A good night's sleep.

SIXTEEN

Raymond cut the Renault's engine and rolled silently to a halt. Predawn fog had formed over the nearby river and was now rolling over the town of Leuven.

"That's it," Leba Fani said, pointing toward a small sign a half block away. Raymond strained his eyes, piercing the fog to read the sign: FELTNER AND SONS. "The loading dock is in the rear. We go down that alley."

He nodded and they both stepped from the car, locking it behind them. From the trunk Leba took a small toolbox. Raymond lifted a four-foot bundle carefully wrapped in heavy blankets and twine.

Wordlessly, they moved down the alley and turned into a second. It led them behind squat, two-story shops with graying bricks and dirty windows. Leba counted off the rear entrances under her breath, and came to a halt.

"Here."

"No regular rear door?"

"No, only the big one, there on the loading platform."

Raymond nodded and climbed the few steps with the woman right behind him. Carefully, she helped him set the bundle down, and then opened the toolbox. She handed him the tools as he asked for them.

"There is no quicker way?" she asked, nervously watching him dismantle the lock mechanism.

"Yes," Raymond said dryly. "We could just blow it apart or break one of those windows out. Then we could just leave a sign when we leave, telling them we dropped by to plant some explosives."

"I just asked," she replied tartly.

It took nearly twenty minutes before they could raise the door enough to move beneath it. After making sure that all the pieces of the lock were carefully laid out on the concrete of the loading dock for reassembly, they moved inside and lowered the door behind them.

"You go first with the flash," he said, hoisting the blanket-wrapped bundle to his shoulder, "and keep it shielded."

Noiselessly, they moved toward the interior of the building, weaving their way around furniture by the light of the narrow pin spot.

"It must still be on the first floor."

Raymond grunted behind her and they descended to the lower floor. The air below was thick with the smell of varnish and other ingredients for the refinishing of furniture.

And then they saw it, sitting dead center in the large workroom, a light dust cover over its gleaming top.

So often had they rehearsed the procedure, they now set to work by the numbers.

Carefully they removed the blankets from the pedestal leg Raymond had carried in from the car. As he compared it to the leg already on the table, Leba set out the tools they would need. This done, she wheeled over a small padded jack and set it in place under one side of the table.

"Did you mark the jack?" he asked. "We must leave everything exactly as it was."

"I did. Do they match?"

"Perfectly. Whoever the lathe man is that Hassan used in Paris, he's a genius to make such a perfect duplication from just a photo."

Leba jacked up one side of the table while Raymond went to work on the leg.

It was just as he had hoped. The Feltner and Sons workman, because of the need for speed, had used modern screws instead of wooden dowels and plugs to repair the leg.

Carefully, he removed the braces and then went to work on the leg itself. When it was off, he laid it beside the copy and compared them again.

Perfect, on the outside.

The only difference was in the fat, top post of the copy. Its center was hollowed out a full foot down into the leg. Inside this hollow a thin lead container had been inserted.

By the time Raymond had satisfied himself that the copy was perfect, Leba had already unwrapped the equivalent of two pounds of Gelemax. Together they kneaded it in their hands and then molded it to fit in the lead container.

As each cartridge of the plasticlike explosive went into the container, the wrapper went into the toolbox.

This done, Raymond inserted the detonator and strung out the lead wire. He then sprinkled turpentine-soaked wood shavings over the Gelemax and tamped them down.

"Ready?"

He nodded and took the batteries, watch, and receiver from her. Hastily he duplicated in the top of the leg the detonating device he had already planted in the roof of the castle.

When a grease-and-garlic-smeared cover had been

placed over the wood shavings, he gently squeezed the batteries, watch, and tiny receiver down in the hollow.

"Perfect fit," he exulted. "Give me the aerial wire!"

With the aerial wire attached, they both reset the leg. Raymond screwed it on tightly and reattached the braces.

Using the tines of a fork squeezed together, he poked the wire in the tiny space between the top and the connecting side boards.

Through the center of the table, beneath the top, there was a half-inch modern steel bar. It had been added years before to combat warping and reduce the strain on the wooden dowels originally used to hold the whole together.

When the aerial wire was attached, the steel bar acted as a perfect conductor for the signal.

When the jack and dust cover had been replaced, Raymond checked the table one more time.

"Well?" Leba asked impatiently.

"It will take more second-guessing than I think they are capable of to figure it out. Let's go!"

It took only five minutes to reassemble the lock on the loading door.

False dawn was just breaking when they got back in the Renault and headed north toward St. Vith.

Halfway there, Raymond stopped for gas.

"You have the proper coins?"

"Yes," she replied, already heading for the pay phone inside the station.

It was picked up on the first ring.

"Gussman?"

"Yes."

"It is done," Leba said, and hung up without waiting for a reply.

• • •

In England, in the Cotswolds, Harvey Raymond was pouring his first cup of tea of the day.

It was five minutes before the hour of seven.

As he did every morning, he slipped from the cottage and walked through the brisk air to his study. Inside, he warmed up the receiver and set the frequency. When the antenna was cranked up, he sat behind his desk and sipped the tea.

He fully expected to be back in the kitchen in ten minutes, fixing his breakfast of eggs and sausage. He was positive everything was going well. There would be no transmission this morning.

But there was, at seven sharp. He saw the needle jump once across the dial. By the time it had settled back to zero, he had lunged from his chair and killed the receiver. He then put it on internal power and activated the computer.

Thirty seconds later he was staring at the unscrambled message on the screen:

AMERICAN AGENT CARTER A MISS IN LONDON. THREE DEAD, NET LOST. VALKYRIE CANCELED. REPEAT. VALKYRIE CANCELED. IMPERATIVE YOU INFORM JA'IL OF CANCELLATION AT ONCE.

"Damn!" Harvey Raymond hissed, erasing the message from the computer's memory. *With London net gone, how in God's name do I do it? By carrier pigeon?*

He paced for a full ten minutes, going over every possible option. He knew about the hunting lodge in St. Vith; it was he who had suggested it to Leba Fani in the first place. But there was no telephone and no contact left now in Wiesbaden.

He could contact Frankfurt, but that would involve blowing Gerald's cover to far too many people.

Gussman. That was a chance, if he could get in touch with the man. Had he left the girl yet?

Quickly, he locked the study and walked to the house. Ynez was sipping tea in the kitchen.

"Good morning, Uncle," she said and smiled. "Must you work before breakfast?"

"Just getting some air. Listen, my dear, I have to go into the village. I won't be long."

Harvey Raymond's mood was black as he drove, and the dismal, cloudy weather didn't make it any better.

Why, he wondered, did Al-Chir cancel the operation just forty-eight hours from completion? Had something happened to Gerald? . . . to Leba? No, if they had been exposed, there would be no need to inform them of the cancellation.

"Damn!" he muttered to himself. "Damn Al-Chir for never letting the right hand know what the left is doing!"

He parked and entered the small hotel. The proprietress, Mrs. Lang, a short, coarse woman with fat features and quivering hands, headed him off just before reaching the pay phone in the lobby.

"Good day, Mr. Raymond."

"Mrs. Lang . . ." He tried to sidestep her, but one monstrous hip blocked his way.

"Beastly weather, ain't it?"

"It always is this time of year, isn't it? Have to use the phone. Afraid the one at the house is out again."

"The bloody cables is probably on strike, like the ones that lays 'em," she said, cackling.

"Yes, probably so." He scooted around her.

"Would you remind Ynez that we've bridge this afternoon?"

"Yes, yes, I'll do that."

The contact number in Brussels answered by machine: Code Red. That meant they had either gone under or been caught up in a police net. Normal. They were probably hauling in every foreigner within five hundred miles of the castle.

Gussman's number in Frankfurt was out of order. That meant he would have already gotten out of the country.

Harvey Raymond would have to go himself. He called Gatwick and got a seat on the ten o'clock flight to Brussels and then rang Ynez.

"I'm afraid I'll have to go to London for the day, my dear."

"Oh, Uncle, on such short notice, and in this weather?"

"Can't be helped, I'm afraid. I'll probably be gone the night. See you tomorrow."

He hung up and dashed for his car. Halfway there, the cold air filled his lungs with pain, making him crouch down and rest to get his breath.

Getting too damned old for this bloody business, he thought, finally reaching the car at a walk but still gasping for breath.

Between the pain in his chest and his mind filled with thoughts of how much he must accomplish in the next few hours, Harvey Raymond didn't notice the dark blue Bentley and the white Ford Cortina.

They traded places behind him all the way across the A40 and on south to Gatwick.

Carter paced, smoking one cigarette after another. He was white hot with anger, but there was little he could say or do to defuse it.

Reinbold sat behind the desk, calmly talking to the woman in low, modulated tones. The woman herself, Ilse

Baunstaffer, sat in a high-backed leather chair stiff as a ramrod. Her jaw was set, her face was stark white, and the tissue in her fingers was torn to shreds.

Carter's instincts had been right. Over breakfast the woman had been all nerves. He had persisted. It hadn't been a pleasant job, but his common sense had told him that something was radically wrong.

When she had mentioned her daughter three times in one sentence, he thought he might have it.

A few phone calls and a little more browbeating and he got it, or at least part of it.

"Your daughter is not at home. She's not at school. The school told us she's visiting you. She's not here, Frau Baunstaffer. Where the hell is she?"

And then she blurted it out. Her daughter had been kidnapped.

Reinbold had jumped right on it. Police, intelligence, and antiterrorist squads had been alerted in four countries. At that moment, three thousand men were searching for Therese Baunstaffer.

But Carter wanted the *why* of it.

"What did they demand, Ilse?" Peter Reinbold asked for the umpteenth time in his quiet voice. "It wasn't money, was it?"

"No."

"What was it, Ilse?"

"They wanted me to help them."

"To do what?"

"They haven't told me yet."

"Bull," Carter growled, leaning forward until his face was inches from hers. "What did they have you do? We've got to know. We'll find your daughter, but we've also got to know what you've done!"

She broke down again, her face falling into her hands.

"I can't tell you! They will mutilate her, possibly kill her!"

"You've got to tell us." Carter's face was livid now and his voice was a menacing growl.

"I can't . . . I can't!"

She was on her feet screaming back at him now. Reinbold was around the desk in an instant, calming her, getting her back into the chair. When he had accomplished this, he nodded to Carter and the two of them moved into the hall.

"Well, the good-cop–bad-cop routine isn't getting us anywhere," Carter said, lighting yet another cigarette and hating the taste.

"It sure as hell isn't. But I can't blame her too much, though. That girl is her whole life."

"Al-Chir could be blowing sand," Carter said. "At the last minute he doesn't come and we've already got a bomb planted."

"Anything's possible," Reinbold agreed, nodding, "but the last word is, he's on his way."

"Do we have any chance of finding the girl?"

"A fair one. They must have her close at hand, probably on the German side of the frontier."

"Colonel . . . Colonel!"

They both looked up. A young BfV aide of Reinbold's in civilian clothes was running down the hall toward them, his face flushed.

"Yes, yes, what is it, Dietrich?"

"The main switchboard just got a call from Frau Baunstaffer's landlady in the village. You're not going to believe this, Colonel . . ."

"Dammit, man, I won't have a chance to disbelieve it until you tell me!"

"The mayor of Trier just called her. A young girl claiming to be Therese Baunstaffer walked into his office a half hour ago, claiming to have been kidnapped. She gave him the number."

"Send one of the choppers over there at once. Have her picked up and brought here."

Carter was already running back to the office and Ilse Baunstaffer.

Carter drank coffee and stood by, scowling as Sergeant Tom Ebert took the old antique apart piece by piece. There was no one else in the room.

"You're sure you don't want to split?" Ebert asked.

"No."

"I'm not kidding. This thing might have an extraction detonator on it."

"I've got faith," Carter said, and moved to the hot plate for more coffee.

"Got it," Ebert suddenly whispered.

Carter didn't pour. He whirled and moved back to the table. The sergeant had his head up under the side boards, so Carter couldn't see his face.

"Where?"

"Somewhere in this leg. Crank that jack up, but go easy . . . one crank at a time."

The palms of Carter's hands were sweat-slick as he grasped the cold steel of the jack handle and pumped it once.

"Again . . . slow, very slow."

Carter did, and watched, dry-mouthed, as Ebert slowly bent the leg and slid it from beneath the table.

"Well?"

"It's cool," the man sighed. "Radio-controlled activation from somewhere outside. It activates the watch, and at a certain time lets the juice through to the detonator."

Gingerly he pulled the metal tube from the center of the

Gelemax and held it up, smiling.

"Now the stuff's just like Silly Putty."

"How close would the transmitter have to be to activate that thing?"

"Mile and a half, two at the most."

"Make me out a full report, everything, in writing."

Carter was already running toward the door and his car.

The girl was twice as calm as her mother as she sat, sipping coffee in a long, terry-cloth robe answering their questions.

"I really didn't know where I was, but I could see smoke far off below me, through the trees. I just kept walking until I found myself in the town. It was Trier."

"All right, Therese," Carter said, sliding onto the coffee table across from where she sat on the sofa. "You say there were three of them?"

"Yes. Two of them left last night, late. They were foreign, Turkish, I think. The last one was German, I'm sure of it. I think his accent was Bavarian."

"And he left this morning, before dawn?"

She nodded. "He came in several times during the night, but he never checked the ropes. That's why he never noticed that I had been soaking them in the water pitcher."

"How did you know to do that?" Reinbold asked curiously.

"I saw it once in a movie," she said with a laugh. "By the time I heard his car drive away, I had them loose enough to slip off."

Carter stood and moved to the window. He didn't like the smell of it. But he didn't know why.

"Therese . . ."

"Yes?"

"You say there were two phone calls?"

"Yes. One last night before the two Turks left, and one this morning before the German left."

Carter turned to Reinbold. "Anything on the cottage where she was held?"

"Nothing . . . no personal items, no fingerprints. It was rented about five days ago by a tall, attractive blond woman. She paid for a month. We've got a description, but I doubt if it's going to do much good."

"I doubt it too," Carter grunted. "Therese, did you hear anything they said to each other, or anything the German said on the phone?"

"No, I'm sorry, nothing on the phone. And the only thing they talked about to each other was me. The two Turks wanted to rape me, I think, but the other one wouldn't let them."

The telephone rang.

Carter looked at Ilse Baunstaffer. Therese had mentioned rape as if they had only wanted to brush her teeth. The mother looked as if she were going to faint.

"Nick, London."

He grabbed the phone like a long-lost friend. "Yeah, Carter here."

"Nick, Jarvis Whitney. Your man got another squirt at seven sharp this morning, and moved."

"Where?"

"He called his niece from the local hotel and told her he was going to London for the day. We got it on the tap. MI5 followed him to Gatwick."

Carter could feel the adrenaline surging. "Where?"

"Ticket for Brussels on the ten o'clock flight. You know Vars Lychek?"

"Yeah. Used to be CIA Brussels."

"Still is. He's alerted, got a five-man, three-car crew waiting at Brussels National."

"Get back to him. Tell him I'm on the way." He hung up and turned to Peter Reinbold. "I need one of the choppers."

"Be my guest. Something?"

"Harvey Raymond's on the way. Let's hope he's heading for Ja'il."

In the courtyard he found a jeep and driver to take him to the chopper pads. At the outside gate, he met Ebert in another jeep coming in.

"Got the report, but it isn't typed," the young demolition expert called.

"Is it written?" Carter asked.

"Yeah, but my handwriting's terrible."

"No sweat, I used to be a cryptographer."

He grabbed the sheets and motioned the driver on with a wave.

SEVENTEEN

The cars were good. One was a battered old Renault dressed up like one of the free-lance mini-cabs that littered Brussels. Another was an ancient Ford Cortina, and the third a big Bentley complete with chauffeur.

"We'll use the Bentley as a control car. Also, if he hits it on foot, we have room to spare for men to work from."

Vars Lychek was a tall, solidly built man, but with oddly narrow shoulders. He wore his graying hair in a crew cut and constantly had a pipe stuck in his jowly face. All these things, plus his tweedy dress, gave him the appearance of an ex-Marine who had turned into a university professor.

"They pick him up yet?"

"Yeah. No baggage, so he zipped through customs. He's at the cabstand now."

"Damn," Carter hissed. "It would be too much luck if Ja'il were in Brussels. Any hint from London that he tagged the MI5 people at the airport?"

"None. A Miss Russell is with him. She's at the cabstand now. She'll follow until we pick her up."

Radio Main crackled from the mounting behind the front seat. "Vars?"

"Yeah, Ken, go ahead."

"Subject took a cab. He's headed downtown."

"This is Vince in Two. Got him out of the main gate."

"Chuck, let's go . . . but stay far back."

The Bentley purred forward and in no time they were on the wide thoroughfare leaving the airport.

"MI5 agent is in a cab between us."

"Got you, Ken. Trade places with Vince. Does subject look nervous?"

"Don't think so."

The next twenty minutes was nothing but seesaw talk. Finally they hit the downtown area around the Grand-Place and circled.

"Subject decabbing on Maison du Roi. MI5 woman agent a block behind. She's hit the bricks."

"Vince, is he walking?"

"Yeah, a good clip on La Montagne, heading your way."

"Vars, this is Ken. I picked up MI5."

"Keep her with you for the time being, Ken," Vars said. "A couple looks more natural."

"Will do."

"He ducked into the Royal Windsor."

"Chuck, take a right and park, fast," Vars barked, and turned to Carter. "There's a side entrance."

The Bentley had barely halted when, through the smoked glass, they saw Harvey Raymond exit from the side entrance to the hotel. He paused, looked briefly up the street, and then started walking at a rapid clip in the opposite direction.

"He's heading back into the Grand'Place," Vars said. "If we drive in there, he'll spot us."

Carter grabbed one of the walkie sets. He stuffed the thin battery pack inside his inner pocket, clipped the mike to his tie, and put the earplug in his ear.

"I'll walk him," he said, leaping from the car.

He started up the opposite side of the street from which Raymond was walking, giving the man plenty of leeway and barely keeping his head in sight.

"This is Vince. We're parked. Subject is just passing us head-on. Jesus, he's staggering . . . his face is white as a sheet. The bastard looks sick!"

"Carter has him on foot."

"Carter, Vince."

"Yeah," Carter breathed toward the mike on his tie.

"Head down La Madeleine—you'll run into him. And you won't have to hurry . . . he's barely moving."

"Got it."

A block later, at the intersection of Duguesnoy, Carter saw him. The man's face was white and he wasn't moving too steadily. Now and then he would pause, lean against a building for support, and shake his head.

"This is Carter. He's heading for the train station, and you're right, he looks like he's on his last legs."

Harvey Raymond couldn't understand the dizziness he felt. It had started at Gatwick and gotten worse on the plane.

Now he had a sudden shortness of breath and occasional chills.

But he had to follow procedure. He was sure he wasn't being followed, but procedure was everything, especially when it was Gerald and Leba who would suffer if he led someone to them.

Just ahead he saw the huge brick and concrete building

with the familiar logo and the words Gare Centrale above the entrance.

He could make it once he made the last evasion and could sit down in a cab.

Carter had stayed over a hundred yards behind the man. But when he saw him head down the stairs toward the express tracks, he sped up. He knew he would have difficulty reaching the subway-type train if one came immediately.

He reached the platform just as the quiet, sleek train was pulling in. Raymond was moving toward one of the doors as the cars pulled to a stop.

"Nick, this is Vars. Look to your right!"

Carter did. The CIA agent was standing with a crowd about fifty yards down the platform to his right. Vars gave the sign that if Raymond boarded the train, he would board with him.

The Killmaster understood. It would be his job to stay on the platform in case Raymond tried to evade. He got change from one of the machines, and waited.

He watched Raymond board, and farther down the platform he saw Vars step into the train.

Just as the doors were closing, Raymond quickly stepped back through. Vars had no time. Carter stayed by the change booth, watching the old man in the mirror of a cigarette machine. He seemed hesitant about his next move as he stood staring up and down the empty platform.

"What's happening down there? This is Vince."

"Vars is on the train, southbound. Subject is heading back to the street."

"I see him. Ken!"

"I'll pick up Vars at the Grand Sablon station."

Carter headed back toward the street. On top of the steps he craned his neck to peer over the heads of the moving people.

"Vince, Carter. I've lost him."

"Turn left from where you are, hit the intersection, cross, then left. It's a little-bitty street called Rue Perot."

"Got it," Carter said, and took off at a fast pace. When he hit Rue Perot he turned left. There was no sign of Raymond.

"Vince, I don't see him."

"It's a bunch of small car alleys in there. You're on your own, buddy. I go in there driving, we blow it."

Suddenly a female voice came through the set. "Mr. Carter, this is MI5 Russell. I am at Rue Perot and Rue Samand. Subject just went into a pub called Le Pub. Quaint, eh? Turn left at the next block and you'll see the sign."

Carter did as he was told. At the corner he couldn't spot the MI5 woman, but he did see the bar.

"Water, please, just water. I'll pay for it."

"There is no need for pay, monsieur. You are ill?"

"No, no . . . just a little pain."

But it was more than just a little pain, and Harvey Raymond knew it. He had almost blacked out twice in the railway station. Now he could hardly get his breath, and the recurring pain in his chest was constant.

Too much excitement for too many years.

But not now, he thought. *Why now?*

The water came and he sipped it slowly, gratefully. It helped, a little. He became aware of people around him, at the bar, in the booths, people coming in, going out. He stared at them, through them. He was searching for a telephone.

The misty film that had formed over his eyes, the pains in his chest, the dizziness. They all told him he wasn't going to make it.

Ynez.

He would have to call Ynez. Gerald would curse him for it, but there still might be a way to keep the truth from her.

He stared harder, trying to focus his eyes.

Le Pub was a small café that had tried to model itself after an English pub, as had so many in Brussels. It consisted of a large rectangular room housing a bar, a dozen or so stools, and a few tables and chairs against the opposite wall. A large mirror ran the length of the room behind the bar. In a corner, mounted above the bar, was a television set.

No one appeared to notice Carter as he entered. Several men were seated at the bar drinking and watching the television. A few men and women sat at scattered tables. Raymond, seated on a stool near the door, was ordering from the bartender. It was not a good surveillance situation. Only three stools were unoccupied and two were right next to Raymond. Carter was tempted to take the one farther down the bar, but decided instead on one of the tables along the wall.

The moment he had ordered a beer he guessed it had been a bad idea to come in at all.

Raymond's watery eyes were focused right on him and they weren't wavering. The suit Carter was wearing was obviously American or English, as was the tie. On top of that, he had forgotten to take the two-way plug out of his ear.

He sighed as he paid for the beer. It had been a long day. Hell, a long week.

When the waiter moved out of the way, he saw that Raymond had zeroed in on him. The man's glassy stare was riveted on every move he made.

The Killmaster couldn't be sure, but he was guessing that he had been made.

Just then, he sensed rather than saw the woman bearing down on him from his right.

"Hello, darling," she said, brushing her lips over his cheek and then standing by the booth as if for inspection.

As Carter stared at her, he tried his best not to look perplexed. She was about twenty-five, about five-five, and about a hundred and twenty pounds. Her head was bare, her hair golden yellow, soft and wavy and not cut short, but falling almost to her shoulders. Her skin was smooth and creamy, and her mouth was full and delicate and softly alluring, and she had a small nose with just enough tilt to it to make it provocative. She had a well-curved, full-hipped body and perfect, nylon-sheathed legs. She was wearing a tailored gray flannel suit, and carried a large black leather shoulder bag and black gloves.

"I'm so sorry I'm late, darling, but you know hairdressers . . . everything has to be just so."

She slid into the booth, and as she kept chattering it dawned on Carter. The woman clasping his hands and nuzzling his neck with her nose was Russell, MI5.

He glanced at Harvey Raymond. The man had lost all interest in them.

"I'm just glad to see you," Carter sighed.

"I thought you would be," she replied, and then lowered her voice. "He's getting a handful of change from the bartender."

"Does he look like he's leaving?"

"Yes."

"Then let's fly the coop ourselves," he murmured, dropping a bill on the table and heading for the door with her in tow. "Vince?. . .Ken?"

The replies came at once.

"He's coming out . . . track him."

"Got him. He's backtracking, opposite direction from you."

Carter and the woman walked faster, took a corner, and headed around the block.

Two minutes later, Vars Lychek's voice came back on. "He's heading back for the train station."

"Come on!" Carter said, and they broke into a run.

In the next few minutes, his estimation of the woman went up several points. As they ran, she removed the blond wig and fluffed her real, dark brunette hair. Next she shed her suit jacket, reversed it to a deep burgundy, and put it back on again.

By the time they hit the Boulevard L'Impératrice a hundred yards from the station, she was a different woman.

"Good show," Carter said. "You stay close, I'll lay back. There he is, heading into the station!"

'She nodded and picked up her pace, slipping on a pair of dark glasses. Carter slowed and began to amble. This time he hoped Raymond would take a train.

There were six pay phones just inside the entrance to the station. Harvey Raymond lurched into one and closed the door behind him.

He punched coins into the slot and began to dial. He had to do it by feel because it had become impossible to shake the mist from his eyes. Also, the pain in his chest was like a vise now.

On the tenth ring, he remembered: Ynez would be at the

hotel in the village playing bridge with Mrs. Lang and her other fat friends.

He got an operator to get information in England. It took nearly fifteen minutes to get the number and ring through. By that time, he knew.

He could barely breathe and he was blacking out.

"Crown's Inn."

"Mrs. Lang, this is Professor Raymond . . ."

"Oh, Professor, Ynez said you'd gone up to London. How's the—"

"Mrs. Lang, I must speak to Ynez at once."

"Oh, Professor, you don't sound—"

"Dammit, woman, put my niece on the line at once!"

"Well, I never . . ."

It was only a few seconds, but the wait seemed interminable.

"Uncle, is anything wrong?"

"Yes and no. Listen, Ynez, I want you to go to Gerald at once."

"Gerald? Uncle, what's wrong?"

"Don't ask questions, Ynez, just do as you're told . . . and quickly. Do you have your passport with you?"

"Yes, I always carry it."

"Good, you won't even have to go back to the cottage. Now, here is what you must do."

He told her to fly out of Gatwick to Brussels and rent a car. Then he gave her explicit directions for reaching the hunting lodge in St. Vith.

"And that's all you want me to tell him . . . 'Valkyrie is off'?"

"That's it, and hurry! You must hurry, Ynez—it is vitally important!"

"Uncle, you sound ill. What—"

"I'm fine, Ynez. Hurry!" He hung up and painfully brushed the perspiration from his face with a sleeve. It was a chore, a struggle, to push the folding door open.

When he did, he stepped from the booth and the final, chest-tightening pain began.

Carter was at the newsstand. Down toward the tracks he saw Vars Lychek. Two other agents were near the door, and Russell was two booths down from Raymond. Carter only hoped she was able to hear snatches of the conversation.

"Nick, he's coming out. Jesus, he's going down . . ."

Carter whirled. Raymond was on the floor, gasping, holding his chest. Russell was already bending over him and a crowd was gathering.

He broke into a run and shouldered people aside. "Make way, make way, I'm a doctor."

He glided to his knees beside Raymond just as Russell looked up and shook her head. "He's dead," she whispered. "Looks like a heart attack."

By that time, Vars and his men were with them. "What happened?"

"Dead," Carter said. "Use your clout. I want a look at everything on him . . . clothes, wallet, everything."

He took the MI5 woman aside by the elbow.

"Did you hear anything at all?"

"Not a word. He barely whispered."

"Damn."

Carter darted into the same booth Raymond had used.

"Operator, a call was just made from this number. Can you tell me where the call went? This is a police matter."

"I'm sorry, sir, we wouldn't have that information, and if we did, we couldn't give it out without written—"

Carter slammed the phone down and stepped from the booth. An ambulance had already arrived. Vars Lychek moved to his side.

"I talked to a friend, local gendarme. No problem on the personal stuff."

"Good. Itemize it and leave out nothing. Here's a Luxembourg number where I can be reached."

He started to move away, and Russell, the MI5 agent, took a few steps with him.

"Sorry."

"Not your fault," Carter said. "I just wish you had supersonic hearing."

He was already running for a cab. It was a guess, but he thought he knew what had suddenly brought Harvey Raymond from England.

EIGHTEEN

They had abandoned the Renault two miles before the frontier and walked across on snowshoes. Both were fit, so it was steady going with only a few short stops for rest.

Now they were about three miles from Schloss Valkyrie and descending through the thick forest.

The light was changing even as Raymond glanced up through the dark, bare branches of the trees. The sun was already half down behind the western crest of the mountain far in front of them on the other side of the valley. And from the center of the valley, the craggy hill rose like a stone needle with its tip the fortress.

The whole area was flooded with red. It would be a half hour to dusk, and then another hour until dark.

The timing was perfect.

They climbed another hundred yards and then descended again. A few moments later, Leba caught up with him and grasped his elbow.

"There, where the smoke is rising!"

Raymond only nodded and veered to the left. Twenty minutes later they stopped just inside the trees and discarded the snowshoes. The heavy hardware was dismantled and stored in their backpacks. They carried the pistols in their belts under their coats.

Raymond squatted and brought a pair of high-powered binoculars up to his eyes.

Leba had chosen well. The small château was far from the main road, accessible only by a rutted, narrow lane. As the crow flies it was about two miles straight across from the castle. Even from there Raymond knew he would have a perfect view of one side and the front of Schloss Valkyrie.

They regained the path and walked the rest of the way down.

The house stood on a rise amid flattish ground separated from the rutted dirt road by a low stone wall that could be jumped over. This they did, ignoring the rusting gate.

It stood back fifty yards from the wall without so much as a bush or tree in front of it. But there were trees behind it, thick, as far up the mountain as the eye could see.

It was two stories, built long and low except for two gabled rooms, one on each wing.

"What do you think?"

"Perfect," Raymond replied. "There is more than enough room on the front lawn for Raab to land the helicopter."

They walked up the stone steps leading to the wide porch. The porch itself was wood and creaked slightly under their feet. The door was massive, oak. There was no electric doorbell, but rather an old-fashioned manual bell with a handle that had to be turned to produce a ring. The only sound they could hear as the bell died out was the ticking of a big clock beyond the door.

Suddenly, French doors were opened directly above them and a tall woman in a severe black dress stepped out on the balcony. Her dark hair was pulled back in a tight knot and, with the dark glasses she wore, she resembled the old-time notion of the traditional schoolmistress.

"What do you want?"

"I'm afraid we've had an accident. Our motorbike veered off the lane and now it's mired down. I wonder if I could use your phone?"

"I don't believe in telephones. They are a nuisance. Don't have one."

Gerald Raymond already knew this—as well as the woman's name, Berta Kirkmann, and the answer to his next question—but he forged on. "Then, I wonder if your husband could give me a hand?"

"My husband has gone to hell. You'll have to help yourselves. There is only myself and my son."

The woman started to step back into the room, but Raymond called up again. "I wonder if my wife could wait in the house while I fetch help from the village. She's hurt her leg, you see, and it is bitter cold."

The woman's stern features got sterner as she looked from Raymond to Leba.

"Please, my leg is very painful," Leba said in her best little-girl voice.

The woman seemed to hesitate, but then she said, "One moment." The doors closed.

Raymond pulled the pistol from his belt and held it just behind his right leg. When the huge oak door opened, he stepped forward, shoving the muzzle into the woman's stomach.

"Where is your son, Frau Kirkmann?"

The woman screeched and arced the talons of both hands toward his face. But she wasn't fast enough and Leba struck like a snake. The side of her hand thudded into the woman's neck, and before she could right herself, Leba had both her arms pulled painfully behind her up to the shoulder blades.

"What do you want? For God's sake, please leave us alone!"

"We need the use of your house for just a few hours, Frau Kirkmann," Leba said. "Now, where is your son?"

"Go to the devil!" Another guttural scream as Leba ripped the wrists upward.

"Where is he, you hag?"

"Upstairs, the right wing, second door. He's napping. Don't hurt him!"

"I assure you, madame," Raymond said, moving up the stairs, "the only harm that can come to you will be your own doing. Put her in the cellar!"

He entered the room without a sound. The boy was sleeping peacefully, only his dark curly head showing above the quilt.

"Alfred?" He shook him gently by the shoulder. "Alfred, wake up!"

The eyelids fluttered and lifted. Two jet-black eyes stared up at Raymond and widened. "Who are you?"

"A friend of your mother's, Alfred. She needs you down in the wine cellar. Come along."

They were in the conference room, standing around the now repaired and reinstalled antique table. Peter Reinbold and Carter silently watched Sergeant Ebert finish his measurements of the room and then scratch out his calculations. It seemed to take forever.

Finally he looked up from the jumbled pad. "Fifty-fifty."

"I like layman's terms, Sergeant," Carter rasped, "but could you be even a little more succinct?"

"Sure. Two pounds of Gelemax, given the size of the

room, the proximity of the people in it, and the area of the initial concussion, you'd have a fifty-fifty chance of knocking everyone off. I'm not saying you wouldn't have quite a few walking wounded, but there's a fifty-fifty chance that the blasts wouldn't kill everybody."

Carter glared at Peter Reinbold and resumed pacing. "I think that nails it. The table's a smoke screen, a decoy. I think there's another bomb."

"Oh, c'mon, Nick," Reinbold said. "Don't look a gift horse in the mouth. We've nailed it."

"Bull. Ja'il wouldn't be satisfied with a fifty-fifty chance. He's too good, too experienced, and too ruthless. He'd want a *total* body count or he would consider the mission a failure."

"You can't be sure of that, Nick."

Carter stopped by the window. "I'm as sure of it as I'm sure he's out there somewhere, watching . . . waiting. Ebert?"

"Yeah?"

"What would have been the risk for Ja'il that the dogs would have sniffed out the Gelemax through the turpentine and the treated grease?"

"Pretty slim."

Carter whirled. "But there would have been a chance?"

Ebert shrugged. "Yeah, a slim chance. Had the whole thing been encased in lead or steel, there would have been no chance. But if he had done that, the blast would have been less effective."

Carter gave Reinbold another long stare, and the German threw up his hands.

"What the hell, even in the assassination business there has to be a margin for error."

Carter stomped to the table and sat. "Not the way Ja'il does it."

"Christ, Nick, the man is human!"

"I don't think so. Therese Baunstaffer escaping from her kidnappers. A seventeen-year-old girl? Bull again. These guys don't make those kinds of mistakes. No, Peter, the table was a blind. There's another bomb somewhere, and I think Ja'il is just waiting to explode it."

"Point," Reinbold said. "You're telling me this Gerald Raymond would blow up Hassan Al-Chir, the man who gives him his orders?"

Carter mashed out his cigarette and looked from one man to the other. Until now he had kept the theory to himself, but now he felt it was time to voice it.

"Harvey Raymond got a squirt transmission at seven o'clock this morning. He went into the little village near his cottage to make a call out of the country. He didn't get an answer, so he hightails it to Brussels."

"To make an eyeball contact," Reinbold said.

"Right. And I think that eyeball contact was with Ja'il. When you have a hunter deep in the bush with no way of communication, that's the only way to contact him."

"But—"

"Let me finish," Carter said, holding up his hand. "Let's suppose the squirt to Raymond was a message telling him to get to Ja'il and stop the Valkyrie kill."

Slowly, Reinbold's face widened with understanding. "And Harvey Raymond has a heart attack, so he can't get to Ja'il."

Carter nodded. "That's my guess. That would mean Ja'il doesn't know Al-Chir is going to be in here. He'll go ahead with the blow."

"*Mein Gott.*"

There was a knock on the door and an aide stepped into the room. "Colonel . . ."

"*Ja?*"

"Major Franholtz on the line from Wiesbaden."

"Excuse me."

Reinbold left the room and Carter cruised to the window. Down in the courtyard, another limousine was discharging another VIP and his entourage. It would be full darkness in another half hour, and by then they would all be in the castle. And tomorrow morning, by ten o'clock, they would all be in this room.

Carter hoped they would all still be alive by ten-thirty.

Gerald Raymond chose the large room in the west wing gable to set up his equipment.

It was a big round room, with windows in every direction but one, that wall stark white plaster with a fireplace in it. An oak settle stood sideways before the mantelpiece, and a black oak staircase, not large but graceful and finely carved, ascended along the rear of the right-hand wall. The dark red tiles of the floor, though uneven with age, had been scrubbed until they had almost ceased to be dull. There was an antique spinning wheel in one corner and a grandfather clock in the other.

But most of all, Raymond was conscious of the atmosphere he breathed, an odor peculiar to such old houses. It wasn't unpleasant, but a combination of a faint dampness, the smell of the polish used on oak, the smell of the old wood itself. It was reminiscent of a schoolroom, the more so as this particular room was lighted by only one electric bulb hanging from the central beam.

Raymond hummed as he set up his transmitter, the battery-powered booster, and strung the antenna. All in all, it would be a very pleasant room in which to spend the next fifteen or sixteen hours.

When he was finished with the equipment, he pulled a chair next to the largest window facing Schloss Valkyrie and adjusted the binoculars.

Beneath them, his sensual lips curved in a smile. The limousines were still arriving. Before long they would all be inside.

Behind him he heard Leba enter the room. She would be bringing them up some food.

"Did you check for any other way out of the cellar?" Raymond asked.

"Yes, it's secure. What do you see?"

He lowered the glasses and turned to her, smiling. "The roof . . . boom."

She, too, was smiling as she set the tray on a table, stood, and pulled her sweater over her head. "I recognize that smile."

"I knew you would," he replied, meeting her halfway.

"Ebert?"

"Yes, sir?"

"Figuring that there is another bomb, and figuring that Ja'il is using the same equipment in the second one . . ."

"I'm way ahead of you," the sergeant replied. "It's like I told you before . . . maximum two miles, and I mean not many feet over that. And he would have to have a fairly clear shot at that . . . not too many trees, and no mountains. That signal is ground wave, like a radio signal on low frequency. It doesn't skip well at short distances."

Carter moved to the other side of the room and gazed across the valley toward the forested mountains.

"I know you're out there, you bastard," he hissed under his breath. "But where?"

Behind him, Peter Reinbold burst back into the room. "Nick, our people found the explosives dealer."

"Gunter Bretoff?"

"*Ja*. He'd carved himself out a makeshift home in one

of the old river caves north of Wiesbaden."

Carter held his breath and let it out slowly. "Did they take him alive?"

Reinbold smiled. "Better than that. Major Franholtz took him alone so he could have a private interrogation."

It was Carter's turn to smile. He knew only too well the kind of "private interrogation" the man had been put through. They were playing real hardball now, and there wasn't time for patty-cake-type games.

"Did he talk?" the Killmaster asked.

"He did. Franholtz gave him one hell of a deal: if he talked, he could walk out of the cave alive. Nick, he made a Gelemax sale five days ago . . . to a blond woman. The description matches the woman who rented the cottage where Therese Baunstaffer was held."

"Bingo," Carter whispered. "How much Gelemax?"

"Ten pounds."

Carter looked at Ebert. "Two pounds in the table."

"I'd say," the sergeant replied, "that eight pounds of Gelemax in the right place would just about put this room —what was left of it—right down there in the lake."

"Peter, I want topographical maps, leases, tax records, everything you can get me about land and buildings for two miles around this place, and a profile on the residents."

"A half hour," the German said, and bolted for the door.

"And one other thing. That custodian . . . the old man?"

"Zigmann?"

"Yeah. How long has he lived in this valley?"

"Eighty-three years. He was born here."

"Get his ass up here." Reinbold went out the door and Carter turned back to the window.

"I'll get you yet, you bastard."

NINETEEN

Ynez parked in the driveway, got out of the car, and stood for a moment studying the hunting lodge. It was dark and there were no signs of life.

"Gerald?" she called, and reacted with a start when her call was answered by the guttural hoot of an owl.

At last she summoned the courage to walk forward and up to the door. She expected no answer, and got none.

"Gerald . . . it's me, Ynez."

The lodge was spooky, and there was no end to the night sounds coming from the surrounding trees. She ventured around to the side, as far as she could go in the headlights of the rented car, and rose to the tips of her toes to peer into a window.

The place looked empty, with sheets for dust covers over the furniture and a general aura of musty abandonment.

Was Gerald expected to arrive? But Uncle Harvey had told her to hurry. Perhaps Gerald had arrived and then gone into St. Vith for dinner.

Ynez decided to do the same. She herself hadn't eaten

all day. If she didn't run into her cousin in St. Vith, she would eat, and return later.

It was a short drive, and twenty minutes later she was sitting in the dining room of a charming hotel in the center of the village.

"Would mademoiselle care for an aperitif?"

"No, thank you, just tea, please, and . . ." Ynez ordered and the woman left. She folded the large, ornate menu and set it to the side, but the picture on its face caught her eye.

So did the large bold letters above it: VALKYRIE.

"There we are . . . cream?"

"Yes, please. Uh . . . what is this?"

"Oh, that's Schloss Valkyrie. It's our biggest tourist attraction, just over the frontier in Luxembourg."

"A castle?"

"Yes, it is quite spectacular. You should see it while you are here," the woman said. "Your food will be here shortly."

She bustled away, and Ynez picked up the menu again.

It couldn't be just some coincidence. Uncle Harvey had said, "Valkyrie is off." What did it mean? Her uncle and Gerald were always involved in some mysterious business deal. This one must be at this Schloss Valkyrie.

Perhaps that's where Gerald is right now, she thought.

The food came and Ynez began to eat. When she finished she would go back to the hunting lodge, and if her cousin still hadn't arrived, she would drive across the border to this Schloss Valkyrie.

The old custodian, Zigmann, was a gold mine of information. He knew everyone for miles around, and their ancestry back for at least two centuries. He also knew every house, every building, and probably every tree on every piece of land.

But his vast knowledge of the area and the people had also proved to be a detriment. He insisted on reiterating every detail before going on to another.

It was taking time, too much time. But right now he was their best bet.

Meanwhile, Sergeant Ebert was closeted with Ilse Baunstaffer, going over every minute detail of work done in, on, and around the castle since her arrival. There was an outside chance he could come up with something.

Carter left the custodian with Peter Reinbold, and made his way to the third-floor suites where the VIPs had been housed with their personal bodyguards and entourages.

He was gambling that he had one last ace-in-the-hole to play if nothing else worked.

"Hassan Al-Chir?" he asked an armed guard in the vast hallway.

"The suite at the end of this hall."

A dark-faced mountain of a man with onyx-black eyes answered his knock.

"My name is Nick Carter. I am associate head of security. I want to see Hassan Al-Chir."

"Wait here."

The giant moved through the second door of the alcove into the main sitting room of the suite, and a clone took his place.

He was back in less than a minute. "Come with me."

Carter didn't know what he had expected, but it wasn't what he found.

Hassan Al-Chir was tall, gaunt to the point of emaciation. So much so that the suit he wore looked terrible and hung on him ill-fittingly. His lips had a bluish cast, and he was unable to hide the palsy in his hands.

So this, Carter mused, *is the most feared terrorist in the world.*

But the cynicism Carter felt was somewhat blunted when he looked into the man's eyes. They, like the livid scar on the side of his face, burned with an intensity that belied the obvious sickness that had invaded the rest of the man's body.

"Mr. Carter, we meet at last. How many years have you been trying to kill me?"

The man's voice was low and sonorous. It was heavy with the sound of command and authority. He didn't offer his hand and neither did Carter.

"Too many, Al-Chir, far too many."

"I assume you are not here to welcome me, so what do you want?"

"I know that Gerald Raymond is Ja'il."

Only Al-Chir's right eyebrow raised slightly. "I am afraid the significance of that escapes me. I have never heard either name."

"What about Harvey Raymond?"

A shrug. "The same."

"Then let me bore you with a little story," Carter growled. "Harvey Raymond left England this morning. I believe he was on his way here. I think he was coming here to tell Ja'il to call off an assassination attempt. I think he was doing this on your orders."

The smile crinkled the scar. "You say this Raymond was in England? I haven't been in England for years."

Carter's jaw clenched and he had to pause to get a grip on himself. One quick thrust, a blow to the windpipe, and the man would be dead.

Ah, he thought, *a consummation devoutly to be wished!* But hardly feasible.

"Harvey Raymond died of a heart attack this afternoon in Brussels. I think he died before he could get to Ja'il."

Damn the man, Carter thought, *not even the flick of an*

eyebrow this time. The man was as cold as ice.

"I leave it up to you and your people, Carter, to provide adequate security. If you do not, and anything happens to me or any of the others, the embarrassment will be yours and the German government's."

"I could call off the conference," Carter said.

"You could. It would be a sign of further intransigence on your sides' parts. In fact, I would almost welcome it."

I know you would, damn you, Carter thought. *A monkey wrench in this meeting is all you want anyway.*

"Do you think, Mr. Carter, that I am afraid to die?"

"No, I know you're not afraid to die. Especially if you can take a few others with you in the process."

Carter turned on his heel and walked out.

There were two heavy trucks and one car in front of her at the frontier. Ynez couldn't understand it. She had driven across Luxembourg several times in the past. It had always been a completely open frontier.

What was going on now that required all this security?

She had half a mind to turn around and go back to St. Vith. Because of a flat tire and all the holdups, it was nearly two o'clock in the morning. Surely, if Gerald were at Schloss Valkyrie, it would be too late to see him now.

At last it was her turn.

"Papers, please."

Ynez handed over her driver's license, the car's rental papers, and her passport.

"Your business in Luxembourg, Fräulein Khadivitt?"

She ruffled. "To see someone. What is going on here?"

"Security, Fräulein. One moment, please."

The uniformed officer moved beyond her lights and conferred with two men in civilian clothes. One of them approached the car.

"Good evening, Fräulein. I am Lieutenant Hermann Vogler, German BfV counterintelligence."

"Good heavens, what are you doing in Luxembourg?"

He ignored her. "Khadivitt. I believe that is an Arab name, is it not?"

Now she really bristled. "It's Iranian, but I am a British subject. Now, would you mind . . ."

"What is your destination in Luxembourg, Fräulein?"

"The Schloss Valkyrie. I'm looking for my cousin. I believe he's there on business."

As she said this, Ynez noticed sudden alertness in the men's faces. Two of them brought their machine pistols up and moved closer to the car.

"And what is your cousin's name, Fräulein?"

"Raymond. Gerald Raymond."

Both doors were yanked open and Ynez, her bag, and her purse were yanked from the car before she could even begin to protest.

TWENTY

Carter awakened at once with the buzz of the phone and glanced at his watch: four in the morning. He had meant to nap for a few minutes and he had slept nearly two hours.

"Yeah?"

"This is Peter, Nick. We're done, and I must say I think I know every nook and cranny and the background of everyone in this valley."

"I'll be right up."

He was already dressed, so just a splash of water on his face and he was bounding up the stone stairs toward the conference room.

"Okay, what have you got?"

"A few improbables that had to be checked . . . recent rentals, basements, cubbyholes. My men did it. Nothing."

"What else."

"Four possible, two probables. Come on over here by the window. I've got the maps set up on that small table."

Carter moved across the room and stood by Reinbold. "Talk to me."

"Okay, far over there to the left. It's a hunting lodge in

those trees. An old man and his wife rent it this month every year. We figure Ja'il could have moved in on them."

"No good," Carter said. "According to Ebert, that many trees would interfere with the signal. Go on."

The other three possibles were good and would have to be checked out.

"Okay, let's get to the two probables."

"One is right up there. You can just see the roof. It's an abandoned ski lodge, boarded up. Zigmann said a bunch of hippies lived there all summer, but they moved out when the cold weather came."

Carter eyeballed it through the binoculars. High, open, well within the two miles, and deserted.

"It's perfect. We'll take it. What's the other one?"

"Move your glasses about a mile to the left on the same line . . . a clear space, two-story house with gabled rooms on both wings."

"Got it," Carter said. "What's the story?"

"Woman named Kirkmann and her little boy. Her husband ran off with another woman about three years ago. She's had it in for the whole world since then, lives like a hermit up there with the boy."

"Anything odd when you called her?"

"Couldn't call, no phone. As I said, she won't have anything to do with the outside world. One of the locals takes groceries up there twice a month. She never comes down to the village."

"That sounds good too. Okay, get some men together. We'll hit 'em one by one at first light."

The intercom phone was going crazy on the conference table.

"Reinbold here. Are you serious? . . . How long? . . . Yes, for God's sake, bring her up here, you fool!"

He slammed the phone down and turned to Carter.

"The cousin, Ynez Khadivitt, is here. They picked her up at the frontier and they've had her in interrogation for an hour."

"Where was she headed?"

"Here, she says, to meet Gerald Raymond."

"Now, Ynez..." Carter said, speaking slowly and calmly to dilute the fear he could see in her face and hear in her voice.

"Nick, why are you here? Is Gerald here?" Tell me what's going on."

"Listen to me. You're sure that's what Harvey told you to tell Gerald, 'Valkyrie is off.' That's all?"

"That's all."

"And he gave you no other place...a building, an address?"

"None. Just the lodge in St. Vith. I went there last night. Gerald wasn't there."

"Ynez, Gerald is here. He's out there, somewhere."

Her head dropped into her hands. "I don't understand all this."

"Ynez, you're not going to believe what I'm about to tell you, but I've got to tell you. And when I've finished, I hope you'll agree to help us, because you might be the key to stopping all this."

Dawn was breaking when the nurse in a starchy white uniform came to get him.

"Herr Carter, she wants to see you. She says she's made up her mind."

Carter moved into the bedroom of his suite. Ynez sat at the vanity, staring into the mirror.

"I'll do it," she whispered.

"We'll leave in half an hour."

He went back to the conference room. Reinbold was waiting with the equipment.

"She'll do it."

"My people have reconned the four possibles. Nothing. Unless he's out there sitting under a tree, he's in one of the two probables."

"Okay, we'll take the abandoned ski lodge first. Get everyone on the bottom floor or in the wine cellar, in case he gets jumpy and goes anyway."

"What about Al-Chir?"

"If anything happens, get him out of here first. Use one of the choppers."

Carter got out of the Audi and leaned back in through the window. Ynez was in the driver's seat, her face drained of color, but determination set in her features.

"All right, you understand this?"

Her red-rimmed eyes blinked yes and she took the walkie from him.

"Just tell him what your uncle told you to tell him, and try to get him to take the radio. I have to talk to him."

She stared into Carter's eyes for a long moment, and then dropped her gaze to the sniper rifle and night scope in his hands. "Will you have to use that?"

"Let's just say it's a necessary precaution and hope that I won't have to use it. Give me about a hundred count to get into those trees over there, so I can see both you and the lodge. Got it?"

"Yes."

Carter moved soundlessly away, counting to himself. When he reached a hundred, he stopped. He had gauged it about right. He was hidden, but he had an excellent view of the front and back of the ski lodge, as well as the approach Ynez would take.

He hated to use Ynez like this, but it was necessary. There was no way of knowing whether Raymond would listen to reason or not.

He heard the soft purr of the Audi's engine, and then tracked her progress along the narrow road toward the abandoned ski lodge. Moments later she stopped. Following his instructions, she got out and left the lights on and the engine running. She walked up the driveway. Twenty yards short of the door, she stopped and began calling Raymond's name. The words drifted back up to Carter on the wind.

He took the scope from his eye and lifted a pair of binoculars to scan from window to window.

Nothing.

After fifteen minutes, he gave up and started jogging toward the car calling Ynez's name. She had barely slid into the seat beside him when the second walkie on his belt, connecting him to the castle, crackled and Ebert's voice came through.

"Yeah, Sergeant, I'm here. What's up?"

"Nick, I think I've got it. The clue came from the log, a repair job on the roof. I went up and found the antenna. I'm going to dismantle it."

Carter's mind went wild. Wherever Raymond was, he was watching. If he saw Ebert on that roof he might just go ahead and blow it.

"Nick, are you there?"

"Yeah, I'm here."

"I told you—"

"Yeah, I know. Go ahead, Sergeant. I'll do what I can to save your ass from this end."

"Got you. Good luck."

"Same to you."

"What now?" Ynez asked.

Carter motioned for her to drive. "We have one more chance."

"Ja'il, there's a car!"

Raymond crawled to his own window and peered over the ledge. He saw the Audi stop and a woman get out.

"Damn," Leba Fani hissed. "I was told that the Kirkmann bitch had no friends, that she never had visitors."

Halfway between the little stone wall and the house, Raymond recognized the figure.

"It's Ynez!"

"Who?"

"Harvey Raymond's niece, Ynez."

"What the hell is she doing here? And there's a man on the roof of the castle! Have they found the bomb?"

Before he could reply, Ynez stopped and called out. "Gerald! Gerald, are you in there?"

"Don't answer her—it's a trick," Leba said, jacking a shell into the chamber of her pistol and readying it by the window.

"Put that down. I don't think she knows we're in here."

"Gerald, please answer if you are there!"

They waited tensely for a full two minutes.

"Frau Kirkmann, are you there? My name is Ynez. I must talk to you if you are in the house. If you don't reply, I have been told to tell you that soldiers will come and search the house."

"I'll get the hag and have her tell them to go away."

Raymond was smiling. "Stay where you are. If Ynez is here, then Nick Carter is around someplace. I daresay he'll know the hysterical Kirkmann woman is lying."

"Gerald, Uncle Harvey is dead. He had a heart attack in Brussels. He was trying to get to you. He called me before he died. Do you hear me, Gerald?"

"What in God's name is the bitch jabbering about?" Leba said.

"Be quiet, damn you!"

"Gerald, he told me to tell you that Valkyrie is off. Do you understand, Gerald . . . Valkyrie is off."

"She's lying! It's a trick!"

"Perhaps," Raymond replied.

"It's off, Gerald, because Hassan Al-Chir is in Schloss Valkyrie. He was invited to the conference. Do you hear, Gerald, Hassan Al-Chir . . ."

"Now I know the bitch is lying!" Leba cried.

She fired right through the window. Raymond saw Ynez spin and fall. He acted on instinct, firing once, hitting Leba high in the chest.

The pistol dropped from her hand and she clutched her bloody front as she turned to face him, shock flooding her face.

"Traitor . . . fool . . . she's . . . lying . . . can't you see . . ."

Blood seeped from the corners of her mouth and she fell forward to the floor.

Raymond ran down the stairs and into the front yard.

Carter had already spotted movement in the front upper window of the house. When the glasses picked up the silhouette of a gun, he had started to move. As he approached from the rear, he monitored Ynez's shouted words on the walkie.

He was almost to the rear of the house when he heard the first shot, quickly followed by another.

That galvanized him. He ran forward and leaped the low wall protecting an outdoor dining area. He could hear more sounds—running feet inside the house—but he didn't stop. He crashed through a pair of French doors and fell to the floor just in time to see Raymond bolt through the front door.

Raymond reached Ynez as she was trying to crawl to her feet. "Where are you hit?"

"I don't know . . . I don't feel anything."

He ripped at her heavy coat until he had it open. He sighed with relief when he saw that the leather and the thick fur lining had deflected the bullet just enough. There was a raw, red burn, but that was all.

Raymond sighed. "It's only a scratch. You'll be all right. Is Harvey really dead?"

"Yes," she replied. "Gerald, did you—"

"He was a good man," Raymond interrupted. "But we both knew there would be an end in all of this for us. I have an idea his will be an easier one than mine."

"It's over, Gerald. Let it be over."

"She's right, Raymond," Carter said, standing behind them on the path to the house. "It is over. Now maybe you and I can talk about Hassan Al-Chir . . . maybe make a deal. It's really him I want."

Suddenly there was a burst of gunfire from the house, the bullets tattooing holes in the snow just to the left of Carter. He dropped to one knee and whirled.

The Killmaster saw the image in the window and sprayed with the rifle on full automatic. What was a woman disintegrated.

Raymond bolted for the front door and Carter swung the rifle down to point at him. "Stop, Raymond, don't do it!"

When the man didn't stop, Carter sighted.

"No!" Ynez screamed, and plowed into Carter's elbow, sending the rifle flying from his hands into the snow.

She didn't even stop in her movement but went on by

Carter and covered the rifle with her body.

The Killmaster took one look at the death grip she had on the rifle, and made his decision. Tugging Wilhelmina from her shoulder rig, he sprinted after Raymond. He took stairs three at a time, following the sound of the other man's footsteps, and moved so fast that he missed the silence when they stopped.

Only when he hit the door of the tower room did he realize that Raymond had suckered him. The man came like a cobra from behind the door. He chopped Carter's wrist, sending the Luger skittering away across the floor.

A steel fist caught him in the center of the gut and his head was slammed against the wall. Everything was shifting from stark white to red and then back to white, when he saw Raymond's face close to his own.

"I don't want to have to kill you, Nick Carter, American, so don't make me."

"It's over, done."

"No, not until I've finished it."

Carter brought his arms up, hard, hitting Raymond's chin into the air. Then he went for the man's throat, but it wasn't there.

The man was fast, maybe too fast.

Suddenly Raymond's hands were at the back of Carter's neck. The man's forehead was battering his face. He felt himself slipping, and then the battering ended.

He was lying on the floor, looking toward the window. As the mist cleared, he saw Raymond connect the wires. He saw the red light on the transmitter begin to glow.

"Don't do it. There's nothing to be gained . . . nothing."

"For me there is."

Then Carter knew that there was no other way. He crawled his back up the wall and, at the same time, tensed his right forearm.

Hugo slipped into his palm. He flipped the stiletto until he held it by the blade.

"Ja'il Rahman, I don't want to kill you, either."

He saw the man's right hand reach for the detonator button.

He reared back and threw the stiletto.

The hand stopped and its twin joined it at Raymond's neck. The razor-sharp blade had pierced his neck so the hilt protruded from one side and an inch of the point from the other.

He turned, staring unbelievingly at Carter, staggered once, and then fell.

Carter tottered to the receiver and held his right hand steady with his left as he turned it off.

"His name was Raab. They spotted him near the helicopter pads, and he was loaded for bear . . . rockets no less. He winged two of my men before they got him."

Carter nodded as Reinbold spoke. He was looking at the two bodies on the floor of the castle's great room.

"How is Ynez?"

"Sedated," Reinbold replied. "Shouldn't we put sheets over them or something?"

"Soon," Carter said.

"Colonel, he's here."

The aide had barely spoken when Hassan Al-Chir walked into the room, flanked by his two bodyguards.

"I will be late for the conference. What is it you want?"

Carter motioned toward the bodies. "Identification."

Al-Chir stepped nearer and looked down. For several seconds he studied the faces, and then turned back to Carter.

"How can I identify them? I've never seen either of them before."

Carter almost laughed. "You mean, after all they have done for you, Al-Chir, you aren't even going to acknowledge them in death?"

"I'm afraid I don't know what you're talking about. I've been told these were terrorists who were going to disrupt the meeting. I have nothing to do with terrorists. I've said that for years. Now may I go?"

"Yeah," Carter growled, "get the hell out of here."

Al-Chir turned stiffly and left the room. Carter turned to Reinbold.

"You can cover 'em up now," he said, and walked out onto the balcony.

The sun was bright. It was a cold, crisp day with clear skies and no hint of snow.

On the roof above the conference room, workmen were repairing the roof where Ebert had removed the bomb.

It had all been for nothing.

"Think anything will come from this conference?" It was Reinbold at his shoulder.

"No. Not a damned thing," Carter replied.

"Damn, all this for nothing."

"Isn't that the way it usually is?" the Killmaster said. "A lot of sound and fury, and damned little substance."

He headed down the stone stairs to find Ynez.

DON'T MISS THE NEXT NEW
NICK CARTER SPY THRILLER

PRESSURE POINT

It was well past midnight. The winds had picked up. The temperature had dropped ten degrees. In the black fatigues, with minimum clothing underneath, Carter was cold and uncomfortable.

He had crawled down the rock face a foot at a time. It had taken the best part of an hour. The rock had torn his hands. The chalky deposits of seabirds had attacked his nose and smeared the black cloth.

He had stopped to check the sentry a few times with the glasses. The man's image grew more distinct. He was tall and looked strong. He was dressed in an olive green uniform with a crest of some kind on one shoulder.

As he got closer, Carter had some luck. The guard was relieved by a smaller man. It would have helped to know how long between shift changes. No matter. This man had just come on duty. Carter figured it would be at least four hours before anyone checked on him. Long enough.

He was within a hundred feet. The last part would be the most dangerous. He couldn't carry his gun or knife in either hand. He needed both for crawling.

Slowly he closed the gap, aware of the scraping of his fatigues against the rock. The sound wasn't carried to the sentry. The crashing of waves against rock drowned out any noise.

When he was about fifty feet away, Carter saw that the man carried a sniper rifle over one shoulder instead of the submachine gun he expected. The man alternated between sitting, his back against the cliff, and pacing the shelf of rock that was his station.

He was like sentries the world over. He was bored and uncomfortable. He undoubtedly wished he was anywhere but there. His mental attitude was probably the same as his fellows. Why here? What the hell was there to see? A stupid, worthless job.

The man's state of mind made Carter's job easier. Almost too easy. After more than an hour of crawling and the concern for his vulnerable position, when he finally crept up behind the man and delivered a karate chop to his neck, it was an anticlimax.

He was wrong. The small man was like a hard rubber ball. The blow that would have floored most men left him unaffected. He swung the rifle stock-first at Carter and missed by inches. The wood shattered against the rock face. Again, the noise was absorbed by the pounding of surf against rock.

They stood facing each other like fighting cocks. Carter had his weapons, but he needed the man whole and ready to talk; the capture would have to be hand-to-hand.

The rock slab was probably fifty feet by twenty. Next to it, an opening in the cliff's face loomed black and menacing. Carter would have to explore it later, but first he had to subdue this small tiger.

The man in the olive uniform tried a blow with his left foot that would have been devastating if Carter hadn't ducked. In turn, as he bent under the blow, he delivered a chop to the man's ribs and heard bone splinter.

Pain creasing his face, the smaller man, extraordinarily strong for his size, tried a blow with his right foot. The result was the same. Carter countered and delivered another slam to the body. The sentry now had cracked ribs on both sides of his chest and he hadn't touched his taller opponent.

Carter was concerned that the struggle was going on too long. Someone might come out of the cavern at any moment. Even above the sound of the waves, the noise of the fight might carry to the interior. He moved under the next charge, swung around, and grasped the smaller man in a choke hold. He held it for twenty seconds until the guard's full weight pressed against him.

Carter let him drop. Time was against him. He pulled the leather case from his pocket and fumbled with its clasp with cold hands.

It held a half-dozen color-coded syringes, and Carter had been well trained in their use. The two yellow ones were harmless: a few drops would put his prisoner out for an hour—all he needed. The two green syringes were for interrogation. They could elicit the truth to all questions or fry a brain beyond redemption, depending on the dosage. The red syringes were lethal, causing a bloodless, silent, quick death.

He took out a yellow syringe, purged it of air, and stuck it in the guard's neck.

—From PRESSURE POINT
A New Nick Carter Spy Thriller
From Jove in October 1987

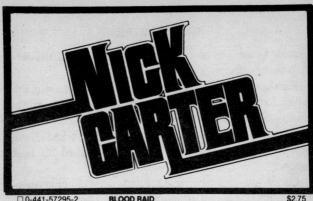